Edie
and the
Box
of
Flits

DISCARDED

KATE WILKINSON

illustrated by Joe Berger

Piccadi
PRES

For my mother, who listened to my earliest efforts at storytelling with extraordinary patience (often as I jumped up and down on her bed), and who gave me and my brothers a love of books.

> *This train is about to depart. Please stand clear of the closing doors.*

The screeches and squawks of a dozen birds bounced off the walls of the tunnel. Just out of reach of their sharp, nipping beaks, the family hurtled along in a ragged line, trying to escape.

'Faster,' said the oldest boy at the front, his head no bigger than a matchstick and his wings whirring like a tiny windmill in a storm.

Up ahead the tunnel divided into two.

'Take the left turn,' shouted his sister from just behind him. They shot to the left and disappeared round a bend. Within seconds the screeches began to fade. It was clear that their pursuers had gone the other way.

'Let's stop,' gasped the youngest. 'Just for a minute.'

They landed on an electricity junction box just beside the train tracks. The youngest did a quick head count.

'Where's Flum?' he said, his voice suddenly panicky. Only minutes before she had been there flying behind them.

'FL-UU-M?' he called back into the tunnel.

There was silence. Flum had disappeared.

Chapter One

Found: three umbrellas, one scarf, an electric guitar (purple), a pair of boots and one wooden box (locked)

It was rush hour. The train rattled and hummed as it made its way through a tunnel deep in the ground under London. The air smelt of old chips and damp raincoats, and passengers sat facing each other on their way home from work, school or a trip to the shops.

Edie Winter stared at a boy sitting directly across the carriage from her.

The boy had red hair like her own, only his was gelled up into tufted spikes and hers hung down her back in two thick plaits. A school tie was stuffed into his jacket pocket and his legs were criss-crossed in front of him like oversized scissors. His thumb was skating back and forth across the screen of his phone as the stations

3

of the London Underground slipped past the windows behind him.

Edie could tell he'd been in secondary school for a couple of years just by the easy way he'd stuffed his tie in his pocket. There were lots of boys like him at her new school; Year Nine boys with gel in their hair whom the girls in her year talked about. She looked down at her own school uniform. The jacket was still so big that only the tips of her fingers peeped out of the sleeves and the corners of her shirt dug into her neck. Dad, who was sitting next to her, had insisted on looping her school tie into a tight V at the collar.

'Even a storm couldn't dislodge that knot,' he'd said, patting her on the head.

I might as well have 'New Year Seven' stamped on my forehead, Edie thought.

At least it was half-term. A whole week without having to wear a tie or walk aimlessly around the playground watching Naz and Linny talk loudly with their new circle of friends.

The brakes screeched as the train arrived at Marylebone Station. The carriage doors opened, letting out a breath of warm fuggy air, and the boy snatched up his rucksack and bounced off.

Edie could see that he did this all the time. The London Underground didn't faze him. He knew his way

4

around the maze of stations and tracks that snaked right across the city.

So did she.

Dad had taught her the names of every line and every station on the whole network. His job at the London Transport Lost Property Office meant that the Tube trains were almost a second home to her. She could even spell 'Piccadilly' without pausing for breath. She wondered if the boy could do that. '"Picc-a-dilly". Two "c"s, one "d" and two "l"s!' she chanted to herself as the doors snapped shut behind him.

Then the boy's face appeared at the window of the train. He pressed himself up against it, trying to look down at the row of seats he had just left.

That was when Edie noticed the box.

It was placed squarely on the seat just beside where the boy had been sitting. It was a wooden box about the size of a large shoebox with a lid, and next to it was a carrier bag marked *Jumble* with a pair of old wellingtons inside. He must have forgotten them, but it was too late. The train began to move forward, gathering speed, and the boy's face disappeared, left behind on the empty platform.

The train rattled on past five more stations as they headed south towards the end of the line where an abandoned electric guitar and several umbrellas were waiting to be picked up. Edie liked these journeys with her dad collecting odd items that had been dropped or forgotten in the rush of London life and reuniting them with their owners.

The box and the boots sat there ignored by all the other passengers who were bent over their phones or reading the free newspapers that were left in piles by every station entrance. Eventually, as the train passed Lambeth North, Edie nudged her dad in the ribs.

'I think someone's left that box on the seat. There was a boy. A teenager. He got off a while ago.'

Dad looked up from his paper and stared at the seat opposite. The train slowed down and pulled into Elephant and Castle and the carriage began to empty.

'How long has it been sitting there?'

'Nine stations,' said Edie. 'I counted them.'

'We'd better take it with us then,' said Dad. The last collection of the day was waiting for them upstairs in the ticket office. After that, all they had to do was take everything back to the office in Baker Street.

'Can I carry it?' asked Edie.

'I suppose so,' said Dad.

He stood up and hooked the 'jumble' bag with the boots over his arm. Stuffed into his pocket was a red scarf he had found draped on a bench at Kensal Green.

Edie picked up the box and wrapped her arms round

it. The box was lighter than she had expected. It was old and a little dusty and it smelt of earth, but the wood felt smooth under her fingers as if many hands had opened and closed the lid.

'Come along then,' said Dad, walking briskly along the platform.

*

When they reached the Lost Property Office back in Baker Street Benedict was waiting at the reception desk. He was nineteen and new to the team. His hair flopped over his eyes and he wore skinny black jeans and T-shirts with slogans on. Today his T-shirt read: *Always Be Yourself Unless You Can Be a Unicorn.*

He jumped up as Edie and Dad came through the door.

'Ta-dah!' he said as if giving them a welcome fanfare.

'Just a few more items to register, Benedict,' said Dad, handing over his trawl of missing things.

Edie clung to the box. 'Dad, can I please just look inside?'

She rattled the lid, but it was stuck fast. Locked.

'No time, Edie. Benedict will sort it out and pass on the information to Vera.'

'I can help,' said Edie, 'I know what to do.'

'No, Edie. It's late and we have to get home,' said Dad. 'Maybe that boy will remember that he's left it on the train and come here to pick it up.'

Benedict had already begun to write out a label in big loopy writing: *One wooden box. Locked (no key). Found on carriage seat Bakerloo Line . . .*

'Come on, Edie. It's rush hour, remember,' said Dad, walking towards the door.

Edie wasn't listening. As she'd handed the box over to Benedict she could have sworn she felt something fluttering inside.

Chapter Two

Finsbury Park to **Baker Street**

Found: *forty-nine umbrellas, three raincoats and a set of false teeth*

Two whole days had passed since Edie had spotted the box, but now at last it was Monday.

Half-term Monday and no school. Dad had agreed to let her help out in the Lost Property Office.

'The first job is to label all these items,' he said, taking her up to the first floor where there was a spare table.

The weekend rain had produced a pile of almost fifty abandoned umbrellas. Edie was restless and her feet were itchy from sitting at the table all morning. She drummed them up and down on the floor and jabbed another sticky barcode label on a damp umbrella. Water dripped from the gutters outside the window.

Edie was waiting for Benedict to come in for his shift.

All she wanted to do was find out what had happened to the box. Had someone come to pick it up? Had she really felt something flutter?

'Ughh!' Edie said. She rubbed at the glue on her fingers.

The phone rang on the other side of the room and Dad answered it. 'Yup . . . right . . . Oh dear . . . that's nasty.' He put the phone down. 'Poor Benedict has tripped up and hurt his wrist. He won't be in until later.'

Edie turned back to the pile of umbrellas. She felt cross and impatient. Why today of all days was Benedict going to be late?

As she waited for him, thoughts about her new school crowded into her head. It was her first term and already she hated it. A bluebottle buzzed furiously at the window beside her, zigzagging back and forth as it tried to find its way out. Edie watched it as it whirred and fizzed. A small scribble of bad temper.

Edie had the same buzzing feeling inside as if she too wanted to escape. She stood up to open the window, gently flapping her hand at the fly until it caught a gust of air and zoomed away. She noticed a small bird sitting on the windowsill next to her. It was watching her carefully. With its sharp orange beak and bottle-green feathers it wasn't like any of the soft-feathered and timid blackbirds or nuthatches Edie had seen in the garden at home. This bird was bold and determined. It was small and shaped like an arrowhead and its feathers were smooth and shiny.

Edie held out her finger, inviting it to step up, but the bird looked at it suspiciously and didn't move. She studied it, noticing that its beak seemed very long for its head and it had a tiny jagged edge that curved upwards. It almost appeared to be smiling, or was it sneering? For a moment it reminded Edie of a baby crocodile.

She turned to shut the window, but not before the bird had darted through it and onto the desk. In less than a second it had snatched a silver spoon from an empty cup and shot up the narrow staircase behind her.

Chapter Three

Baker Street

The staircase led up to the office of Vera Creech. It was little more than a cupboard with a small window, and next to it, right at the top of the stairs, there was a door that led out to a fire escape. Edie checked the door in case the bird had slipped through it but it was firmly shut.

Vera was sitting at her desk in front of a large computer screen. She sat very upright and her fingers pecked away at the keyboard. Her job was to keep track of all the items of lost property that arrived at Baker Street and mark them up as 'found' if someone claimed them back. She did all this by means of a large spreadsheet on the office computer system that everyone called Sherlock. Today she was tapping in the details of an abandoned set of false teeth.

Dad's card sat on her desk with the words *Being Lost and Found is the Stuff of Life* across the front. Edie knew it was Dad's motto and he'd given the card to Vera as a welcome gesture when she'd joined his team a few weeks before. Edie thought Vera was a bit strange. She wasn't cold exactly, but she rarely smiled and didn't seem to like talking very much.

Edie stood at the doorway looking up at the ceiling. 'Did you see a bird come up here?'

Vera stopped tapping and looked up. She had odd lopsided hair that on one side was cut short and tucked behind her ear and, on the other, fanned outwards like a pleated skirt. Running through it was a streak of blue.

'Up the stairs?' said Vera crisply. 'No. I don't think so.'

Edie edged her way into the room, trying to stop staring at Vera's hair.

She knew that Vera liked birds. A net of nuts hung from her open window and a large crow sometimes perched on the sill waiting for Vera to feed it crumbs. It wasn't there today.

Vera started tapping at the keyboard again, filling in the details of the guitar that Dad had picked up from Elephant and Castle. An eyeglass hung round her neck like a monocle. It looked old-fashioned as if it was something that Sherlock Holmes might have used to study a crime scene.

'A bird came in while I was working and stole a spoon,' said Edie.

'Oh?' said Vera. 'Well, I haven't seen it up here.'

'It was very odd-looking,' Edie went on. 'It had green feathers.' She nodded at the net of nuts. 'It might have been hungry.' She looked outside and could have sworn she saw a flash of green in the plane tree beyond. 'Did it fly out of your window?'

'Are you sure you didn't imagine it?' Vera said a little impatiently.

Edie peeped behind the door, but there was nothing there and she began to doubt whether she had, in fact, seen the bird at all. Perhaps she had fallen asleep for a moment and it had slipped into her mind at the edge of waking and dreaming? She decided to plunge in with the other question that was on her mind.

'Has anyone come in yet to claim a wooden box? It was found on the Bakerloo Line.'

'Who wants to know?' said Vera.

'Well . . . *I* do. It was me who found it on Friday afternoon with Dad . . . I mean, Mr Winter.'

Vera paused and clicked something on her keyboard.

'It was just . . . I think there was something alive inside it,' Edie said and then immediately regretted it.

Vera looked up sharply. 'I see.'

She returned to her screen and seconds later she said, 'No. As yet unclaimed.'

Chapter Four

Found: *five mobile phones, a mountain of odd gloves and a rabbit-shaped alarm clock*

'**D**ad? Can I go and look in the Storeroom at the End?'

Edie had joined Dad downstairs in the basement. The day's haul of lost property sacks had already slipped down the blue post chutes that ran from the ground floor to the basement like a helter-skelter. They were now lined up on the trolley beside him ready for sorting. On the wall above the trolley a poster shouted in large red letters: *We Return What You've Lost.*

'All right, but don't spend hours in there,' he said.

Edie loved the storeroom at the end of the corridor on the ground floor. It was the last of three storerooms and it was where all the oddball, one-off things were shelved.

If, as Vera said, the box hadn't been claimed by anyone, it was sure to be there.

'Stack all the items marked *Unclaimed* in a pile,' Dad went on. 'Time they went to the charity shop. Load of old tat, most of it. Can you find a place on the shelf for this?' He handed her a rabbit-shaped alarm clock that had just arrived.

'I love all the old tat,' said Edie. 'Do you remember that cape, Dad?'

When Edie was still at primary school, a sequinned cape had been handed in to the Lost Property Office. It was made out of a luminous fabric that glowed in the dark.

'I do. It was found on the Victoria Line,' said Dad. 'It was a bit spooky, that cape.'

He had let Edie keep it as after three months no one had claimed it and she had worn it in bed for a week. As she lay in the dark wrapped in its luminous green glow she imagined herself running through the tunnels of the Victoria Line with the cape fanned out behind her like a moon creature's wings. When she showed how it shone in the dark to her two best friends from school, Naz and Linny, they were amazed.

As Edie walked down the corridor to the storeroom she tried once again to push away thoughts about her new secondary school. Right from the first week Naz and Linny seemed different and they had laughed at her new uniform. They'd talked in horrible scratchy whispers about her baggy jumper and oversized school shoes. They'd never made fun of her before, but now that they were in Year Seven it seemed to matter what you looked like.

'Why are you still *so-o* small?' Naz had said one lunchtime. She was already almost a head taller than Edie.

'Did you think getting big shoes would make you grow?' said Linny in a strange sing-song voice. She leant over to Naz to show her a Snapchat picture of a ring of girls laughing and making faces.

Edie opened her mouth to speak but nothing came out. She felt as if someone had pushed her hard and she was falling backwards off a wall that she had sat on for years. She fiddled with the end of one of her plaits. 'I can still run the fastest,' she said.

Naz and Linny looked at her as if she was their annoying younger sister.

'Not in those shoes you can't!' Linny said, and then they had ignored her. They didn't even ask her what she was going to do over half-term.

Edie had decided early on to stop talking to either of them or their horrible new friends and her days at school were largely spent in silence.

The corridor narrowed and Edie stopped in front of

the last storeroom. She unhooked the latch and pushed open the heavy metal door, breathing in the familiar smell of old biscuits. The fluorescent strip lights buzzed into life. There were no windows in the storeroom, as the walls were covered with shelves that reached from floor to ceiling, and there was an old Persian rug on the floor that had been found rolled up at Waterloo Station almost three years before. No one had ever claimed it, but Dad had kept it as he said it gave the storeroom an air of homeliness.

Edie walked along the first shelf, pulling out any items that were marked with the red *Unclaimed* labels. The pile grew – first a child's Pokémon rucksack, then a Mickey Mouse money box, an Arsenal football flag and an egg whisk. She quickly scanned the other shelves, hoping to catch a glimpse of the box, but couldn't see it.

She became distracted by the new arrivals, pressing the alarm button on the rabbit-shaped clock to make its ears wiggle before she found a place for it on the shelf, and plucking at the strings of the purple electric guitar. She was just about to pick up a strange medieval-looking sword, when she heard a tapping sound – sharp and insistent. It was an annoying tap, like a twig against a windowpane on a windy night.

Edie stopped to listen.

There it was again – tap, tap, tap.

It was coming from somewhere high up.

She dragged a chair across the floor and levered herself up until her head was level with the top shelf. She ran her hands along the surface, feeling her way. Her right hand rested on the soft brown felt of a cowboy hat. She pulled it towards her and spun it to the floor like a Frisbee.

Moving further along, her fingers caught in the feathers of a large stuffed bird. She snatched her hand away, thinking for a moment of the bird with the crocodile smile, but its feet were firmly glued to a wooden plinth.

She stopped again to listen. The tapping was over to her left.

Climbing down, she moved the chair along and tried again. Just next to the stuffed bird, her fingers rested on the sharp corners of a wooden box.

She felt certain it was *the* box. Her box. The one she had found on the Bakerloo Line.

Edie scrabbled for it and dragged it towards her. She felt sweat prickling on her forehead as she slid it off the shelf and into her arms. Yes, it felt the same, and she could see Benedict's wobbly handwriting on the brown label stuck to its side, but she could now also see that there were two small panes of glass at each side and the tapping noise was coming from one of the panes.

Edie felt scared and excited. She hadn't been mistaken about that fluttering when she'd handed over the box to

Benedict; there *was* something alive in there. Perhaps it was a hamster with a little wheel for exercise? If it was something alive, it would be very hungry.

Edie weighed up what she was feeling. She knew she could be timid at school and hang back, but all her life curiosity had burnt like the flare of a match inside her. Gripping the box to keep it steady, she stepped back down from the chair.

The tapping became louder and more frantic. Edie held the box up until the pane of glass was level with her face. At first all she could see was a faint yellow glow, but it was blurry, as if someone had smeared the glass with grease.

Her eyes slowly adjusted. A tiny creature was beating its fists against the glass.

It was about the size of Edie's thumb. It had wings that were whirring furiously and a puff of hair that was like the fur on the tip of a cat's tail.

The creature stopped banging and started to wave wildly at Edie. Then, clear as a tiny bell, words began to form.

'I want to come out RIGHT THIS MINUTE.'

Chapter Five

Baker Street

Edie stared at the small glass window and her mouth gaped open. She had to fight the urge to drop the box and run back down the corridor to the safety of the office.

The creature waved again, both arms this time, as if it was flagging down a plane.

'Can you *hear* me?' it said.

Eventually Edie replied in a croaky whisper. 'Yes. Yes . . . I can.' She felt her heart beating fast against her ribcage.

'At last,' said the creature.

'Are you some kind of insect?' Edie asked slowly and quietly. 'Like a moth?'

'A MOTH!' said the tiny voice inside the box. 'Moths have giant flappy wings. No, no. I'm a flit. F-L-I-T.'

'O . . . K,' said Edie. She tried to sound as if she met flits all the time.

'My name's Impy,' said the flit. 'What's yours?'

'Edie,' she almost whispered. The weeks of silence in the playground seemed to have shrunk her voice.

'Speak up!'

'EDIE. Edie Winter.'

Impy gave Edie a hard stare. 'Will you help us, Edie Winter?'

'I-I don't know yet,' said Edie.

'We were hiding in a garden shed and Charlie was helping us,' Impy went on.

'Charlie?' Edie said. 'Do you mean the boy with the red hair who forgot you?'

Impy was getting impatient. 'No-oo . . . That's Ivan. His stupid big brother. Charlie's mother decided to have a clear-out of the shed and Ivan was supposed to take the box to a charity shop.'

Impy pressed a tiny hand to her forehead. 'He forgot about us and left us on the train, and now we've been stuck in this room for two whole days. *Two whole days!* Stuck on that shelf between a cowboy hat and a stupid stuffed owl.'

'Oh!' said Edie. It was quite a speech. How could Ivan . . . have forgotten about them? Meeting a flit was the most exciting thing that had ever happened to her.

'It was me and my dad who rescued you,' said Edie. 'This is a lost property office.'

'Funny sort of "rescue"!' said Impy. 'Leaving us stuck in the dark in here without anything to eat.'

'We don't normally keep *living* things here,' said Edie. 'They usually go to the RSPCA – or the zoo. I-I don't really know what to do with you.'

'How old are you?' asked Impy urgently through the glass.

'Eleven,' said Edie. 'I'm twelve on Christmas Eve.'

'Well, that's fine then,' said Impy. 'You can take us home and we can live with you.'

The idea was mad. Edie knew it was. She should leave the box where it was in the back storeroom and hope that the strange flits would disappear. Yet she also knew that, more than anything else, she wanted to keep Impy all to herself.

She sat down on the chair to steady herself and rested the box on her knees. Swinging her plaits out of the way, she bent her head so that she could look inside more easily.

Impy was still pressed against the square of glass. 'You must help us!' she pleaded. 'We need food and water.'

'How do I let you out?' said Edie.

'There's a button hidden at the back. Press it.'

Edie felt along the back of the box, her fingers sliding across the smooth wood.

'Can you find it?' said Impy through the glass.

Edie scowled and ran her hands over the whole surface, until right in the far corner she felt a small raised button. She pressed it and with a soft click she felt the lid release under her hand.

Edie suddenly felt anxious. Had someone meant to keep the box locked? She rested her arms across the top of the lid and pressed down. What if they were evil creatures? What if she opened the lid and a swarm of strange talking insects poured out of it as hungry as locusts? What if she could never get them back inside again? The idea was terrifying, but it also sent a tiny thrill through her.

The tapping started again – insistent like a miniature woodpecker. Impy was pummelling at the glass with her fists. 'Come ON,' she yelled.

Edie weighed up the situation. Impy *was* quite loud, but she didn't look evil. Slowly she raised the lid.

A sharp gust of air whipped past her cheek and Impy landed on Edie's hand. She was a little bigger than a pencil sharpener and was dressed in a coat crafted from squares of brightly coloured sweet wrappers tied with a piece of parcel string. Her shoes were made from scraps of stitched leather. She folded her wings against her back.

25

Edie had to grit her teeth to resist the urge to swipe her away. If she had wings, she might also have a sting! But she managed to hold her hand still, and Impy sat down cross-legged. They gazed at each other and, after a moment, Impy lay back against Edie's fingers and threw her arms behind her. It tickled.

'Fresh air!' she said in a voice that sounded less impatient and more like the ting of a small bell. 'It was horrible being shut in.'

She sat up and swung her legs round so that they dangled over the ball of Edie's thumb. 'Good to meet you.'

'Ye-es,' said Edie. Although she didn't quite know what she was meeting.

'The first thing is supplies, and then we *have* to go back to the end of the line to meet Jot,' Impy continued.

'Jot?' said Edie.

'He's my brother. Speckle is really missing him.'

Edie felt she was being pulled along a slippery path and couldn't get her footing.

'Who's Speckle?'

'He's Jot's twin. He's in the box.'

Edie looked into the box. It was as if she had lifted the lid on a doll's house and was looking down through the roof. A series of compartments were linked by a maze of small corridors and the whole box was furnished with items that must have been foraged by its thumb-sized inhabitants. The walls were lined with old seed packets. There were beds with jewel-coloured duvets made from scraps of cotton and a bath made out of an old anchovy tin. A couple of Lego bricks provided a table and round it stood a set of stools crafted from bottle corks.

'Charlie gave us those,' said Impy, pointing at the Lego bricks and a miniature skateboard that acted as a sofa on wheels. A bootlace doubled up as a washing line and several small bottle tops, filled with rice, grains, seeds and raisins, sat on the shelf above. Edie was relieved to

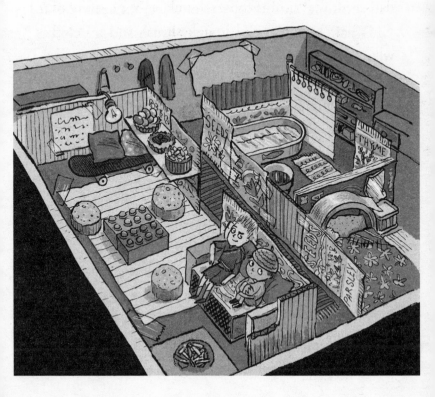

see a jam jar half filled with water slotted into the corner with a tiny pulley system and a bucket on a string.

Right in the centre of the box, in the largest compartment, two small creatures like Impy were seated on a matchbox. They looked like little bendy figures made of plasticine wearing clothes.

'That's Speckle,' said Impy. 'And that's Nid, my annoying younger brother.'

'Hello!' said Nid. He pulled three tiny silver beads out of his pocket and juggled with them, expertly catching and throwing until they were nothing but a shiny blur. Nid's hair stood up like a pastry brush and his clothes were made from the pocket of a pair of jeans.

'Show off!' said Impy.

Edie laughed and her eyes flicked back to Speckle, who was hiding in the shadows of the box. He wore an acorn cup pressed tightly on his head like a miniature helmet, and he gazed up at her with an urgency that she didn't understand.

'What happened to Jot?' she asked.

'He decided to go back and look for Flum and the nut.'

'Flum?' asked Edie. There seemed to be a cast of thousands in the flit world.

'Yes, Flum!' said Impy. 'Our flum. Like mum to you. We lost her in the tunnel when we were escaping the magpins. They came and attacked the Hillside Camp, which is our home. And now she is *missing*.'

Nid dropped his juggling beads and they scattered in all directions, pinging off the walls of the box. Impy ignored him and carried on.

'One minute she was behind us and then she was gone. We think the magpins must have caught her and stolen our nut.' She almost spat out the word 'magpin'.

Edie realised that Impy had a lot on her mind. 'Do you eat nuts?' she asked.

'No!' said Impy, looking horrified. 'Inside the nut is our new baby sister or brother. It's not long until it hatches, and Flum was carrying it. Now the magpins have got that too.'

Edie marvelled for a moment that a baby flit could be hatched out of a nut.

'The magpins have been stealing all the flit nuts,' Impy went on. 'When they attacked the Hillside Camp we flew into the Underground to escape.'

'So this box is not your real home?'

'No!' said Impy. 'We found a safe place in a garden shed by the station at the end of the line, which turned out to be Charlie's garden. Jot told us he would come back to find us at the station, and in the meantime Charlie gave us this box to live in and helped us furnish it and he promised to keep us secret. So we stayed there safe for almost five days until –' her voice became a little indignant – 'until Charlie's mum put us out with the jumble.'

One of Nid's beads catapulted out of the box and hit Edie on the head. She longed to ask more questions. Above all, who were the *magpins*? But she could see that Impy was getting agitated, so she stayed quiet and stared at what remained of Impy's family. They were so extraordinary and yet there were things about them that she recognised. They were not insects, but tiny people with wings who lived in a house, slept in beds and wore clothes. Though they had babies that hatched out of nuts.

Her eyes roamed around the magical scene below her. 'What's in there?' she asked.

She was pointing to a compartment that was full of glittery things – a five-pence coin, a bent hair grip decorated with glass crystals and a broken silver charm in the shape of a lizard.

'That's Nid's room,' said Impy. 'He likes finding forgotten shiny things. That's how we live, by foraging for things no one wants any more.'

Nid stood up on the matchbox and did a forward somersault off the side, landing perfectly.

'He can fly but he chooses not to. He prefers to jump and run.'

Edie was transfixed. She wanted to sit in the storeroom staring at the inside of this magical box for a whole week.

The sound of the four o'clock tea bell jangled in the distance. Dad would be expecting her back in the office, but she couldn't leave the box here, not now she knew what was inside.

Chapter Six

Found: *one gold ring*

'Impy, I want you to meet *my* family. Well, my dad. He works here.'

'Can we go to your house after?'

'Maybe,' said Edie. 'But we'll have to be careful. Someone else might see you.'

'Adults can't see us,' said Impy simply, and she flew up and lodged herself behind Edie's ear in the twist of one her auburn plaits. 'Ivan couldn't see us. That was the whole problem.'

'Now *I* can't see you!' said Edie.

'You can hear me, though!' Impy blew into Edie's ear. A tiny gust of air tickled her earlobe as if it was a pixie feather.

'Agh!' said Edie, laughing. 'Why couldn't Ivan see you?'

'Too old. No one over thirteen can see us.'

'That's weird,' said Edie. 'You can't just disappear when someone turns thirteen.'

'We do,' said Impy.

'But . . .'

It didn't seem fair at all. Edie's twelfth birthday was only a few weeks away, and then she would be in her thirteenth year. She wanted to spend the rest of her life watching flits.

'I like your hair,' said Impy. Edie could feel her clambering up and down the twists of her plait. 'Can I have a swing?'

'OK,' said Edie slowly, and she leant forward and tipped her head to one side so that her plait swung free of her head. She could see Impy clutch it as if it were a giant rope swing.

As she moved her head Impy shrieked. 'Faster, Edie!'

Edie swung her plait to and fro until her neck ached, but she felt something inside that she hadn't felt for a while.

Impy sat upright, breathless with excitement. 'We're going to get along very well. Do you know what your hair reminds me of?'

Edie had been told by her dad that her hair was special and glowed like copper. But she had also been called 'carrot head' by a boy at school.

'Marmalade,' said Impy. 'That lovely dark orange marmalade that Charlie liked to put on his toast.'

'Marmalade?' said Edie. She felt quite pleased with this comparison. 'No one's ever said that before.'

Impy gave the plait a sharp tug. 'Let's get going.'

'Ow!' said Edie, although she was beginning to like having a flit in her plait. 'OK. You can come if you hide in my hair. But the others will have to stay in the box just for now.' She couldn't risk treading on them or losing them between the floorboards.

'It won't be for long,' she said to their upturned faces as she closed the lid.

Holding the box in front of her, she set off back down the corridor and up the stairs towards the front desk. A customer was talking to Dad and becoming quite agitated, so Edie edged round the back of his desk, placing the box on one corner.

'Stay out of sight,' she whispered to her plait, not yet convinced that Impy really was invisible to adults.

The woman on the other side of the desk was wearing an expensive suit and flapping a newspaper to fan herself. Dad was on his hands and knees crawling slowly across the floor towards Vera, who was in the corner of the room wearing her stout black shoes and regulation trousers. Dad said this was a hangover from the long years she had worked in a ticket office on the London Underground.

Round her neck dangled her eyeglass.

The woman spoke in an increasingly high-pitched babble. 'Mr Winter, first of all you've taken six weeks to report back to me that you've found my ring . . .'

'Yes, bit of a mix-up. Vera . . . er, Miss Creech here . . . is quite new to the job.'

The woman ignored him. 'And now you've dropped it and lost it. Or perhaps it's been stolen? Or maybe a mouse has got it? It's not good enough.'

'I had it here this morning ready for you,' Dad said from the floor. 'Vera?'

Vera held up a brown label with a string tie that was marked: *Gold ring. Emerald stone. Found on Victoria Line at Green Park Station. Back of seat.*

'I *know* you had it here this morning ready for me because *you* phoned *me* to come in and collect it. I'd like to see the manager.'

Dad knelt upright and breathed slowly as if he had a pain. 'I *am* the manager.' He pointed to the badge pinned to his lapel. It read: *Here to Serve You.*

The woman looked appalled. There was a silence as Dad resumed his search, crawling his way along the skirting board.

'Benedict!' he called through into the back office. 'We need the broom.'

'All right, Mr Winter,' shouted Benedict. He had

35

just arrived and appeared in the doorway with his wrist wrapped up in a bandage. He waved at Edie with his other arm and retreated into the back office to find the broom.

'You must have a manager,' the woman was saying. 'All managers have managers.'

'Um . . . well . . . she's called Ms Slate. Ursula Slate,' said Dad, shuffling alongside the blue postal chute. 'Please just give me another minute.'

Edie could tell that he was upset. Any mention of Ursula always upset him.

She also knew that recently there had been a high number of items of expensive jewellery reported missing on the Underground, but the items never reached the Lost Property Office.

People were beginning to talk and the *London Herald* had run a banner headline: *Valuable items go missing on the Underground. Is Lost Property Office failing in its duty to find them and return them to their owners?*

If Dad found this ring, maybe the *London Herald* would say better things.

Benedict had reappeared and was pushing an industrial-sized broom around the floor with his good arm. Dust began to cloud up around the woman, like talcum powder around a baby's bottom. The woman coughed dramatically.

Out of the corner of her eye Edie saw
something feathery dart across the room
over Dad's head and perch on top of a filing
cabinet. It was the bird again. So she hadn't
imagined it, but how had it got back in?

'It's a magpin!' hissed Impy.

A magpin? This was the creature
that had attacked the flits. The
magpin cocked
its head and
stared at Edie.
In its orange
beak she saw it
was holding the
gold ring, and she felt
Impy climb down the twists of
her plait and scuttle onto her shoulder.

'Impy,' she hissed.

Impy's wings whirred in her ear as she lifted off and
headed towards the magpin. Edie felt panicked.

'Where's Flum? What have you done with her?' Impy
yelled at the magpin as she fluttered dangerously close to
its beak.

The magpin cocked its head to one side and flapped
its wings, weighing up whether to snap its beak at Impy
or keep hold of the ring.

Impy ducked under its beak out of its sight and dangled from the loop of the gold ring as if she was a circus trapeze artist. The magpin began to shake its beak from side to side.

Benedict clapped his hands together and cried, 'Bird in the house.'

Snatching the broom out of Benedict's hand, Edie swung it up into the air as if it were a lightsabre and charged at the magpin, waving the bristly end. The magpin flapped its wings and took off, landing on the overhead light. Edie swung the broom in a wild circle over her head, shouting, 'Shoo! Get out!'

'Don't!' cried Vera.

Alarmed by the commotion, the magpin flew down, landing briefly on the woman's head before opening its beak to let out a loud squawk and dropping both Impy and the ring. Then it shot through the flap of an air vent and out into the street beyond.

Chapter Seven

Baker Street

'It's gone,' shouted Benedict.

'What on earth *was* it . . . ?' said Dad.

'Maybe one of those nasty pigeons?' said the woman, patting wildly at her head.

'It was a bird and it had the ring,' said Edie, falling to the ground to find Impy. 'Don't move anyone!' She lay on her front on the floorboards.

'Impy?' she whispered. 'Where are you?'

Her eyes frantically scanned the floor, expecting to find Impy, her body broken or trodden underfoot, but there was nothing.

'Who is this girl?' the woman asked from above her. Edie opened her mouth but nothing came out. She had to keep her eyes down.

'She's my daughter,' said Dad, filling in the gap.

The dust slowly settled around them.

'I think this has all gone far enough . . .' the woman said very grandly.

With perfect timing Impy appeared, a little dusty, climbing out of the seam of a floorboard clutching a large gold ring with a green stone in her arms. She held it up towards Edie. Edie silently breathed a thank you and, taking the ring, she allowed Impy to scuttle back up her plait.

'Is this what you were looking for?' she said to the woman, standing up and opening her hand.

'Ahh!' the woman gave a gasp. She squeezed the ring back onto her finger and her eyes brimmed with tears. 'Mr Winter, may I congratulate you on your sharp-eyed daughter?'

Dad smiled weakly.

Edie felt Impy whir past her hair and relodge herself in her plait. No one seemed to have noticed the flit, although Vera was looking at her very fixedly from across the room and was fiddling with the eyeglass round her neck.

'You should put *her* in charge,' the woman went on, before opening her purse and handing her a twenty-pound note. She gave Edie a wink, revealing an eyelid that was shaded with a slick of peacock blue, and then she swept out of the office.

Dad threw his hands up in the air. 'Well done, Edie. Sherlock Holmes couldn't have done much better!

You saved the day! Vera, mark up the computer entry as "Claimed".'

Vera left to go back to her office.

'*I* saved the day,' said Impy indignantly from her perch just behind Edie's ear.

'Not bad!' said Benedict, smiling, and he picked up the broom and walked out after Vera. 'Strange bird, though. I'll have to look it up.'

'I was worried that woman would complain to Ursula,' Dad carried on. His boss was particularly keen on order and lists and absolutely no mess anywhere.

'At least you can tell her that you returned the ring,' Edie said.

'Yes. That should put me in her good books for once.'

Dad sat down heavily in his chair, his arm brushing against the box.

'What's this?'

'Oh, it's that box we found on the Bakerloo Line,' Edie said, 'I found it down in the room at the end. No one's claimed it; I checked with Vera. Can I take it home, Dad?'

'Edie, we're supposed to wait three months. That's the rule. It's only two days since it arrived!'

'Please, Dad. It's just an old box.'

'Huh!' Dad said. 'What's so special about it then?' He pulled it towards him to have a look inside.

Edie felt as if someone had wound her up into a tight spring. This was the moment. The real test of the flits' invisibility.

'It's nothing much, Dad.' She laid her hand protectively on the lid.

'Come on, Edie.'

'He can't see us,' whispered Impy.

Edie pressed the button at the back and opened the lid. Speckle was sat on the matchbox drawing and Nid was busy polishing one of his five-pence coins in his bedroom.

Dad adjusted his glasses and peered in. The flits turned to look up at him, each tiny face a pale disc the size of a fingernail. There was a long silence.

Eventually Dad said, 'Strange. All that miniature furniture. Maybe someone kept tiny dolls in there or small furry animals like you used to? Those tiny furry things that you used to push around the room in a campervan with a little tent on top.'

'Ye-es, Dad,' said Edie. She tried to sound bored but inside she felt elated. He *hadn't* seen the flits!

'So can I take it home?'

'No, Edie, you cannot. Three months and that's the rule. It doesn't belong to the LPO until then, and at that point it will most likely go to the charity shop.'

Edie felt Impy tugging at her plait. 'Please, Dad.'

'No, I'm sorry. Ursula would never forgive me if she found out.'

Edie knew she couldn't push it. Dad was already in trouble with his boss for letting an expensive Wedgwood vase slip out of his hands like a piece of soap and smash into a hundred pieces, and then there was the issue of the missing valuables that the Lost Property Office had failed to find.

'I'm taking it back where it belongs. Now get your coat, Edie.'

He clicked the lid shut with Nid and Speckle inside and disappeared back down the corridor with the box.

'Impy,' Edie said to her plait. 'You have to go back too.'

'No I *won't*,' said Impy furiously. 'I've only just got out. What if the magpin comes back?'

'You can't come with me,' said Edie.

'Plee-ase,' said Impy. 'Just tonight. We need supplies. I've got a list. Your dad won't see me. The others will be safe here for one more night and Speckle doesn't like to leave the box anyway.'

Edie hesitated. More than anything she didn't want to get Dad into trouble, but she couldn't ignore the flicker of excitement that bounced about in her chest and ran down her arms to her fingertips at the thought of Impy going home with her.

'OK,' she said finally. 'But you'll have to hide in my pocket.' Impy scuttled down her arm and slid into the pocket of her dungarees.

As they walked to the station Edie said, 'Here, Dad . . . you take the money.' She tried to hand him the twenty-pound note that the woman had given her.

'Certainly not, Edie. It's yours to spend on whatever you like. You earned it.'

Edie could think of a hundred things to spend it on, but one thing stood out.

'Could I get new school shoes, Dad?'

'That's a bit boring, isn't it? You've already got school shoes.'

'Mum bought them two sizes too big for me and they flap when I walk.'

Surprisingly Dad understood. 'Well, that won't do,' he said. 'We'll get new ones tomorrow.' As they waited for the train, Edie opened her pocket a fraction to look inside. Two tiny fierce eyes were staring back at her.

Chapter Eight

Alexandra Park Road

Edie stood beside the draining board in the kitchen, longing for Dad to finish scrubbing the spaghetti pot. He was taking ages refilling the sink with soapy water and rubbing at the sides of the pot with wire wool.

'Can't you go faster?' she said, twisting a soggy tea towel into a knot.

'What's the hurry?' said Dad.

How could he know that a tiny flying person was waiting for her upstairs in her bedroom? Impy had agreed to stay under Edie's bed while she ate supper. In return Edie had promised they would raid the kitchen as soon as Dad had gone to bed. She had left Impy with water and an egg cup of Rice Krispies, but she hadn't intended to be so long.

At last Dad tugged at the fingers of his rubber gloves and peeled them off. 'Now we have to call Mum.'

'I-I've got homework, Dad!'

'It's half-term, Edie. What's got into you? You always look forward to these calls.'

He flipped open the laptop and clicked on Skype.

It was two days since Mum had gone to Finland to look after Granny Agata. Agata was eighty and lived on her own, but she had fallen in the kitchen and needed help.

The laptop beeped and suddenly there was Mum on the grainy blue screen with her hair scraped back behind her ears. She looked tired.

Edie waved. 'How's Granny Agata?'

'Today was a good day,' said Mum, 'She got up for a while and sat in her chair by the window. We could hear the migrating geese honking overhead as they left the lake.'

'Aark! Aark!' honked Dad, flapping a tea towel in the background.

Both Edie and Mum laughed.

'How about you, Edie? Anything exciting happen?'

Edie swallowed hard. She longed to spill out everything to her mother in a tumble of words – how she had found the box of thumb-sized flits, how Impy's wings whirred like a hummingbird's and how Flum and the nut baby were missing, but she couldn't. She almost had to pinch her tongue.

'I helped Dad in the office,' she said instead. 'And I catalogued forty-nine missing umbrellas.'

'Wow,' said Mum, 'I'm impressed.' After telling her about the rabbit alarm clock with the wiggly ears (and avoiding any talk of Naz and Linny), Edie handed the laptop over to Dad.

'I'll see you very soon,' Mum said.

For a moment Edie sat beside Dad as he talked to Mum. She thought of Granny Agata's window in her rust-coloured house by the lake and the geese with their long necks stretched out as they took to the air. Then Impy flitted back into her mind, filling every corner of it, and she hurried towards the stairs mouthing to Dad that she was going upstairs.

Relief flooded through Edie as she peered under her bed. Impy was sitting inside the egg cup, looking bored. She flew up onto Edie's bedside table and crooked one arm onto her hip. 'You took ages.'

'I had to help with the washing-up.'

'What about my list?' said Impy.

'We'll go as soon as Dad's asleep.'

Edie snapped on her bedside lamp so that Impy was standing in a pool of light. They stared at each other. Edie could see Impy's ribcage fluttering in and out as a heart the size of a biscuit crumb pumped blood around her tiny body. Her sweet-wrapper jacket gleamed.

'It's stitched with fuse wire to withstand collisions with insects and hailstones,' she said proudly, and pointed to a tiny badge stitched onto it with the letters *F7*.

'What's that stand for?' asked Edie.

'Foraging. Top set. I can read the train map and find useful stuff in the Underground.'

'Like what?'

'Well . . . wooden lolly sticks to build houses, chewing gum for sticking things together, leftover sandwich crusts for toast . . .'

Edie had so many more questions, but she thought she shouldn't ask them all at once. Impy, on the other hand, was keen to explore. She took off and hovered in the air for a moment with her tiny cobweb wings beating hard, before flitting around the room to look at Edie's belongings. She paused by a photograph of two figures at the beach smiling and clutching a baby. The woman's hair was blown back from her face.

'That's Mum and Dad with me when I was little,' said Edie.

'Where is your flum now?' said Impy.

'She's gone to Finland for a few days to look after my grandmother. She grew up there and she doesn't like London winters much. Too foggy and wet, she says, and not enough snow. She misses the cold. The real cold. It always makes her laugh that Dad's family name is Winter.'

Impy flew on past a string of lights hanging from Edie's wardrobe and peered through the glass of a fish tank that contained two guppy fish. They darted away from the glass and watched Impy curiously from behind a clump of weeds. Then she flew over to the window and stared out into the street. So fish could see flits.

Edie came and stood beside her. She had looked out of this window countless times – at the row of houses with their postage-stamp front gardens and crooked lines of bins. The whole scene was bathed in the orange glow of the street lamps and in the distance they could hear the rattle and rumble of the long freight trains as they passed through London on their way to the ports on the east coast.

They stood there for some time, listening, until the TV went silent downstairs and the rush of water in the bathroom signalled that Dad was brushing his teeth. Eventually Edie heard the click of his light switch in the next-door bedroom.

It was time for the midnight raid.

Chapter Nine

Alexandra Park Road

'Sugar sprinkles,' Impy ordered. 'And more Rice Krispies.'

Edie's bare feet padded back and forth across the cold kitchen tiles as she searched for the items on Impy's list. She found a tub of coloured sugar strands at the back of a kitchen cupboard and the cereal packet was already out on the counter.

'Sunflower seeds and raisins,' Impy went on. 'And some grapes with the pips taken out.'

The grapes were fiddly, but the list carried on: chocolate spread, three digestive biscuits, a triangle of cheese and some wine gums. Impy pointed to a string bag full of walnuts on top of the fridge.

'Can we take one of those for Speckle? As a sort of "comfort nut" to remind him of ours. He used to take care of it the most.'

Edie picked out a small oval-shaped walnut and found an egg box that made the perfect container for the seeds and raisins. She scraped out some chocolate spread into a bottle top and filled a jam jar with water. Then she hid everything in her sports bag and left it by the front door. Soon after midnight Edie padded back up the stairs to the bedroom with a second egg box. She filled one of the egg holders with cotton wool and put it on her desk.

'Here's where you can sleep.'

Impy hovered in the air, whirring in front of Edie's face.

'Do you *ever* sleep, Impy?'

'Not much,' said Impy. 'Flum says I've got a lot of energy.' She landed on the desk and prodded at the cotton-wool mattress.

'Why do you need me to look after you?' Edie said.

Impy folded her arms. 'We have to find Flum and I don't think Jot can do it alone. He's brave in a stupid way. It makes him leap into danger without thinking.'

'Where is he now?'

'Somewhere down in the Underground tunnels, trying to find Flum and all the other missing flits and nut babies, but he will come back for us. He's loyal. I'll give him that.'

Edie was thoughtful. What could she do? The flits were her responsibility now.

'My dad *finds* missing things on the London Underground. It's his job,' she said. 'I can help you to find Jot. Maybe he'll turn up in one of the lost property sacks.'

'Good. Let's start tomorrow,' Impy said.

Edie felt tired. Tomorrow would only come if she slept. She brushed out her plaits and put on her pyjamas. Impy watched from the bedside table and then, as Edie crawled under her duvet, she disappeared.

'Impy?' said Edie.

'Down here.'

Edie looked over the edge of her bed. Impy was in the shadowy bit underneath, tugging at something from between the tufts of carpet. A few seconds later she reappeared, dragging a tangle of cord. Edie recognised it at once. It was a bracelet made from a purple thread of cord and strung with three letter beads: L-E-N.

'What's L-E-N mean?' asked Impy.

'It's just a . . . friendship thing. The L-E-N stands for Linny, Edie and Naz. Linny and Naz were at primary school with me.'

Impy held the bracelet out towards Edie. 'Don't you want to put it on?'

For a moment Edie's fingers instinctively circled her wrist. Then she pulled them away. 'Nah,' she said, and she took the bracelet and stuffed it in the drawer beside her bed.

Impy looked at her questioningly, so Edie changed the subject.

'I still can't believe that anyone who gets to thirteen can't see you any more.'

'Maybe it's because they don't want to,' said Impy. 'Friends become more important.'

'Well, mine won't,' said Edie. 'I don't have any friends now anyway.'

'Things change,' said Impy. 'But first will you help us find Jot and Flum and the nut and get back home to the Hillside Camp?'

'Yes. I will,' said Edie firmly, although she didn't have a clue how she was going to do it.

Impy yawned.

Edie laughed. 'So you do get tired sometimes.'

She offered her finger for Impy to perch on and lowered her into the egg box, so that she could step down and crawl into her egg-box bed.

Chapter Ten

Alexandra Park Road to **Baker Street**

It was a crisp autumn morning and Edie's breath smoked in the air as she left the house with Dad. She kicked at the leaves blowing across the pavement on the way to the Underground. Her sports bag was strapped across her back and Impy was tucked into her plait. A family climbed onto the train at King's Cross, and for a moment the youngest girl stared curiously at Edie's plait. Edie pulled up her scarf to cover her ears and the girl eventually looked away.

They walked up Baker Street beside the red-brick apartment blocks. In the distance Edie could see queues of tourists already forming outside 221b Baker Street where the detective Sherlock Holmes was supposed to have lived. A policeman was standing outside in a Victorian policeman's outfit with a cape, posing for photographs. There was a line of red buses waiting at the lights so Dad took Edie's arm and steered her through the traffic to a shoe shop on the other side.

'What style would you like?' the shop assistant asked as she measured Edie's foot.

Edie wasn't used to choosing school shoes as Mum had always chosen them for her, picking out pairs that were sturdy and hard-wearing with plenty of room for growth. She scanned the racks and pointed at a pair with a narrow strap across the front. At least they wouldn't flap about like two enormous boats.

'Bit dull, aren't they?' said Dad.

Edie looked at him, surprised. Dad was many things, but he was *not* fashionable.

'Go on,' he said. 'Pick something you like. I won't tell Mum.'

Edie's eyes wandered along the racks. The shoes began to get more interesting, and some of them were in a sale. There was a shiny black patent loafer with a tassle and a pair of lace-ups with a pattern of tiny dots snaking over the toes. She tried on the loafers, as she knew that Linny had a pair. She walked up and down the shop determined that they should fit, but they felt stiff and uncomfortable and pinched round the toes. I'll get them anyway, she thought. Linny would be impressed.

She felt a small tug on her plait. 'Look over there,' Impy whispered in her ear.

Right at the end of the line were a very different pair of shoes. They were a bit like trainers but made of leather – sporty with thick soles and long laces that criss-crossed all the way up the front.

'They'll fit,' said Impy.

Edie turned to the shop assistant. 'I'd like to try those, please.'

She walked around the shop, angling her feet this way and that in the mirror. They felt neat and light and they fitted perfectly; Impy was right. Edie felt like dancing.

'We'll take them,' said Dad.

Edie looked at the price tag. Even in the sale they still cost almost £30. 'I'll pay the difference,' said Dad.

Never again would she have to wear the awful flappy shoes with the Velcro fastenings.

'Take the old ones along to Ada's charity shop,' Dad said.

*

Edie could see Ada through the window tipping piles of clothing out of plastic bin liners onto the table at the back of the shop. She picked up sacks of unclaimed clothing and trinkets every day from the Lost Property Office to sell for charity.

Ada came rushing to the door and pulled Edie into the folds of her big flowery dress, smothering her in a waft of overblown roses.

'How are you, girl?' Ada said, squeezing harder.

At last she released her, and Edie was able to pull her old shoes out of the bag. 'Do you think anyone will want these, Ada?' The toes curved slightly upwards like bananas.

'Yes. They'll go soon enough,' said Ada. 'Everything finds a home in the end. I'll put them in the window.'

A clothes basket in the corner made a strange gurgling sound.

'Come and meet Baby Sol,' said Ada. She was a child-minder and usually bought a baby or a toddler to the shop with her.

Edie peered into the basket. A baby was kicking its legs joyfully in the air.

'Play with him, Edie, while I put these shoes on display,' said Ada, and she headed towards the window.

'Hello,' Edie said, and gave the baby a little wave. She could feel Impy shifting in her plait to look into the clothes basket too.

'Daba-da!' the baby said, and beamed back at Edie. She gently tickled his tummy.

'DABA-duh-da!'

'It's HUGE!' said Impy. 'Must have been a big nut.'

'Human babies aren't born in nuts!' Edie whispered.

Impy ignored her and hovered down near the baby's face, pressing its nose with her hand as if it were a tiny car horn. 'Bee-eep!'

'DUB. Duh. Daba-DA.'

The baby clapped its hands together with a shriek of laughter and snatched at the air, trying to catch Impy, who quickly returned to the safety of Edie's plait.

'That baby can see you all right,' whispered Edie. Impy darted down again and gave another beep on the 'horn'. But this time the baby pushed its lip out and started to cry.

'All done,' called Ada from the shop window as the cries rapidly grew in volume.

Impy pressed her hands over her ears and buried her head in Edie's plait. 'Do they always make so much noise?'

Ada hurried over and peered into the clothes basket. The baby was still bawling and its face had turned from pink to red. 'Oh, poor little love,' she said, and picked the baby up to rest on her shoulder. She gently patted its back until the heaving sobs and overheated cheeks subsided and she could gently push its thumb into its mouth.

'What a relief!' said Impy. 'Baby flits aren't half as noisy as that.'

Edie paused to look into a glass cabinet by the door. In among the costume brooches and teaspoons, she spotted some doll's-house furniture. There was a wooden cradle on a rocker complete with a pillow and a patchwork quilt. She decided it would be perfect for Speckle's nut.

'How much is that?' Edie only had fifty pence left in her purse.

'That'll be fine,' said Ada, wrapping it up in newspaper with her free hand. 'I can see what you do with it when we come over next Monday.'

'Monday?' said Edie.

'Yes, it's all fixed. Juniper is coming to stay with me from tomorrow so I'm going to make us all a meal while your mum is away. You and Juniper can have a nice play together. Your dad thought it was a great idea.'

'Right,' said Edie. She tried her hardest to give Ada a bright smile.

'Bub-Bub. DABA!' shrieked the baby as Ada walked back across the shop.

Edie looked away. It was a terrible idea. Ada's grand-daughter Juniper was really annoying.

Chapter Eleven

Baker Street

Found: a copy of Harry Potter and the Half-Blood Prince and a pair of basketball boots

'Look at these, Edie!'
Dad held up a pair of size-twelve basketball boots. 'Don't you think *these* would make the perfect school shoes?' He was pegging missing pairs of shoes onto a washing line that was strung alongside the helter-skelter post chute.

Benedict picked another *Harry Potter* book out of a sack. 'That's the third one this week,' he said. 'Always claimed back, though.'

Edie slipped her feet into the basketball boots. They were so big that she didn't even have to take her own shoes off. She looked like a clown.

'You try, Dad,' she said, laughing.

Dad pulled them on and loosely tied the laces. Padding about, he searched for a basketball in among a bag of missing balls, and after bouncing it a couple of times, he lobbed it down the corridor at Benedict.

Edie felt a tug on her plait. 'The supplies!' Impy whispered, but Edie was distracted by the impromptu basketball game. Benedict held out a wastepaper basket with his unbandaged arm and the ball clattered into it. 'Slam dunk!' he shouted, and Dad drummed his oversized boots on the floor.

There was another tug on Edie's plait. 'What about Nid and Speckle?'

Edie turned to go just as Dad lobbed a football towards Benedict's makeshift basketball hoop. Halfway down the corridor, the office door opened. The ball hit the visitor smack on the side of the head. It was Dad's boss, Ursula Slate.

Ursula wore neat wedge heels and her hair was pulled back into a bun. It was so tightly fixed with hairspray that even the full force of the ball didn't dislodge it. She stared at Dad's shoes. 'Are those lost property?' she said sharply.

'Well, they are . . . but I was just checking they were in working order and –'

'May I remind you that this is not a playground?'

'Yes, Ursula. It was just a silly bit of fun,' said Dad.

'You're supposed to be a manager, not a sports coach.' Ursula stood with her mouth zipped up into a tight line as Dad tugged off a basketball boot and hopped about on one foot. She waited until the basketball boots were pegged back on the washing line, and then smoothed down her armour-plated hair as she unfolded a newspaper.

'We are being accused of not doing our job!' she said indignantly, pointing at an article. 'It seems that there is a very large number of things going missing on the Underground and we are not finding them! I've had a lot of complaints. Be vigilant, team. Be-ee vigilant!'

'Do you think there are train robbers down there? Gangsters maybe? Or pickpockets?' asked Benedict. He couldn't quite keep the excitement out of his voice.

'No need to be overdramatic, Benedict,' said Ursula. 'The question is, are we fulfilling our duties?'

She clapped her hands together as if she was shooing chickens back into the coop and turned to go. 'Everyone, get back to work!'

The door slammed shut behind her. Edie and Benedict

doubled over with laughter, but Dad looked anxious.

'Huh!' he said, gathering up the ball. 'Why does she always appear at the wrong moment?'

Edie felt a sharp pinch on the lobe of her ear. 'Let's *go*!'

Edie picked up her bag. Dad had begun to empty a new sack of lost property that had just slid down the helter-skelter, but Edie could see by the look on his face that his heart wasn't in it. Ursula's unexpected visit had clearly rattled him.

Chapter Twelve

Baker Street

Edie could see from the corridor that the door to the Storeroom at the End was already open and the fluorescent lights were on. Vera Creech was in there, crouched on the floor as she searched for something on the lowest shelf, and Edie could see the eyeglass dangling from her neck.

Edie glanced quickly up to the top shelf and saw that the box was still there. 'Can I help, Vera?' she asked, trying to sound nonchalant.

Vera stood up quickly, banging her head on the shelf as she did so. 'Ah, Edie! Yes . . . I was just checking some details on a new arrival.' She snatched at the rabbit-eared alarm clock. 'Here we are. Just checking how many . . . er . . . ears . . . the rabbit clock has.'

'Most rabbits have two ears, don't they?' said Edie.

She couldn't help feeling that Vera was not telling the truth.

'Yes. Yes, of course. Two ears it is. And what are you up to?'

'I'm just sorting through some of the unclaimed items. Dad says it's time to hand them over to charity.'

'Right,' said Vera.

'Right,' said Edie.

Vera was shifting uneasily from one foot to the other.

'That box you mentioned, Edie?' Vera said. She smiled as if she was trying to be friendly but the smile didn't quite reach her eyes. 'I was just wondering . . . if it was here?'

Edie felt Impy shift in her hiding place deep in the twist of her plait and give it a sharp tug. If she had arrived any later, Vera might have reached the top shelf and found the box.

'I-I . . . don't . . .' Edie began to say.

Just then the rabbit alarm clock whirred and clicked in Vera's hand and its alarm went off, making them all jump. Vera pressed at the buttons on the back, but the alarm continued to ring.

'Ugh! What a horrible noise!'

'I can stop it,' said Edie, and she took it from Vera and flicked a small switch. In the silence that followed she said, 'Did you see its ears move?'

Vera looked confused and seemed to have lost her train of thought.

'Do you want to see a medieval sword? It's not real but it looks good. And there's an electric guitar . . .' Edie went on, trying to think of all the things she could say to distract Vera further.

'Er . . . well, I don't really have time. Things to do!' Vera said, and she left, her shoes tapping rapidly as she went down the corridor.

Edie closed the door behind her.

'Why did she want to know about our box?' said Impy, launching herself from Edie's plait to hover in front of her.

'Well, it *is* her job!' said Edie, lifting the box down from the top shelf, but she too felt uneasy.

Nid was waiting at the pane of glass, perched on the sill like a tightrope walker.

'We've got supplies!' Impy called out.

Edie opened up the sports bag and unpacked the contents of the egg box. She lowered the bottle top filled with chocolate spread into the box and Nid immediately seized it, scooping a dollop of the sweet, sticky paste out with his hand. Edie refilled the jam jar with fresh water and then unloaded all the groceries, placing them in piles round the matchbox. Impy and Speckle carried everything through into their larder, filling thimbles and small glass jars with the Rice Krispies, sugar sprinkles and raisins.

Edie watched as the flit family wheeled a digestive biscuit into the main living room and coated it with a slick of the chocolate spread. Then they sat round the edge nibbling at it as if it were an edible tabletop. Chocolate spread was smeared up Nid's face and into his hair. Edie wished that she could shrink in size so that she could join the party round the biscuit table and scoop luxurious handfuls of chocolate spread into her mouth. Instead she put her hand in her pocket and lifted out the cradle and the walnut. She gently put it down in front of Speckle. Speckle clapped his hands together and tucked the quilt round the 'comforter' nut.

Edie was completely absorbed when the door rattled open. For a moment Edie thought it might be Ursula Slate, but it was Dad coming to check up on her.

'Edie! Vera said I'd find you in here. You're not looking at that box again, are you? There's a lot to do.'

Edie snapped the lid shut and heard the lock click into place. She knew that Impy was still inside, but there was nothing she could do. 'Sorry, Dad. I'm coming.'

'I'm going to make this storeroom out of bounds,' said Dad. 'Put that box away right now and bring those things with you.'

He sounded much bossier than he normally did and

Edie knew that arguing would only make things worse. She put the box back on the shelf and filled her arms with unclaimed items, but she could hear Impy hammering on the glass, her voice tinny and desperate, as she switched off the lights.

Chapter Thirteen

Baker Street to **Alexandra Park Road**
and back to **Finsbury Park**

Found: one shopping trolley

Edie's head was spinning. Dad had given her a long list of 'things to do' and had disappeared down to the basement. She tried to distract herself by sorting through the forgotten pull-along shopping trolleys that were piled into an untidy pyramid. How could she see the flits if they were stuck here in the Lost Property Office? Especially now Dad had made the storeroom out of bounds. Worse still, she didn't trust Vera, who might be snooping about again. She had to think of something fast.

It was Benedict who came to her rescue. He was talking on the phone at the front desk, and beckoned Edie over mid-call.

'There's a lady who lives in Finsbury Park. She left one of those shopping trolleys on the bus, but she's elderly so she can't come and collect it. Could you take it to her, Edie?'

He went to the pyramid of trolleys and pulled out a large floral one. He wheeled it into the middle of the room and stood it upright. 'I know it's a boring job, but I just haven't got time today. There's a queue of people coming in to register missing valuables and asking questions. I've got lots of forms to fill in. Ursula was right. There's definitely some serious pickpocketing going on. Remember: *Bee-ee vigilant*, Edie.'

He pointed to a label attached to the shopping trolley. 'The owner's address is here.'

The shopping trolley looked weird. It was like a sack on wheels that bulged at the front, but it gave Edie an idea. It could give her the perfect cover if she was quick. The owner lived only a short bus journey from her house. She wheeled the trolley down to the Storeroom at the End and, pulling the box off the shelf, she lifted the flap of the trolley and stuffed it inside. She could just hear the high-pitched jangle of Impy's voice, but there was no time to explain anything to her.

Vera Creech met her in the corridor. She looked irritated, as if she hadn't expected to find Edie there, and impatiently tucked a strand of blue hair behind her ear. 'Where are you off to, Edie?'

'I'm just running an errand for Benedict. I should be back in a couple of hours,' Edie said.

Vera peered at the shopping trolley.

'An old lady left it on a bus a couple of days ago. I'm taking it back to her.'

Without waiting for Vera to reply, Edie half ran down the corridor and up the stairs to the front reception. The shopping trolley bumped and rattled behind her as she headed down Baker Street. A man muttered as Edie ran over his foot, and a dog chased after it, growling and snapping at the wheels.

By the station Edie noticed a large bird with black feathers picking over a half-eaten carton of fast food in a rubbish bin. It had a row of bristles at the top of its beak. As Edie walked past it stopped and stared at her with ringed unblinking eyes. It reminded her of the crow that sat on Vera Creech's window. She looked away and hurried past, dragging the trolley after her onto a busy Circle Line train.

*

Five stops and one change later, the bus from Finsbury Park to Alexandra Palace was packed. She could see through the flap of the shopping trolley that the box had tipped onto its side. Three boys got on board at Crouch End that Edie knew from the year above her at school.

'Look at the old lady,' said one, prodding his friend in

the ribs and pointing at Edie. 'Doing a bit of shoppin'?' He shouted at Edie as if she was deaf.

Edie felt her tongue turn to stone and looked out of the window.

At last the bus slipped down the far side of Alexandra Palace and within minutes she was walking down her street.

*

It felt strange being at home alone during the day.

The kitchen smelt of burnt toast and the plates lay in an untidy pile in the sink. Bilbo, the Winters' giant poodle, was asleep on the doormat beside the back door. He spent his days watching squirrels through the dog flap, occasionally bolting out into the garden to herd them up a tree.

When Edie came in he leapt up and stood guard at the flap as if she had caught him sleeping on the job. He looked warily at the shopping trolley, as Edie pulled out the box and set it upright. As soon as she opened the lid Impy whirred up in front of her nose. Inside the box it looked as if a tornado had blown through it. There were sugar sprinkles, Rice Krispies and raisins everywhere and several of the small jars had smashed.

'You locked us in!' Impy cried.

'I had to,' said Edie. 'But I've brought you to my house.'

Impy didn't seem to hear what she was saying. She perched right on the tip of Edie's nose and dug her heels in. 'You must NEVER do that again,' she said. 'You tipped us up and the box is a horrible mess! We all felt sick.'

Edie squinted at her. 'I'm sorry, Impy. But look where we are!'

At last Impy lifted up into the air and looked around the kitchen. Her eyes rested on Bilbo. 'Hrrrmph . . .' she said grudgingly.

Edie was already tugging off the label. 'I've got to go back to the office quickly so I'm going to have to hide your box. Dad must never know I've brought you all here.'

'Don't lock us in again. PLEASE,' said Impy. 'We won't go anywhere, but we're not your prisoners.'

Edie felt a flush of guilt that she had put Dad's feelings before the flits'. 'Of course,' she said. 'I'll leave the box open in my bedroom, but you have to stay upstairs. If Dad discovers that the box is here, I'll be in big trouble.'

She pushed the box under her bed and left the lid wide open. The flits were already hard at work tidying up. Speckle was pushing around a small broom fashioned out of a toothbrush. The walnut was back in its cradle.

All she had to do now was take the shopping trolley back on the bus to Finsbury Park and reunite it with its owner. It shouldn't take long if she hurried.

'Impy,' said Edie as she was leaving, 'please don't let the others out of your sight.'

'I won't,' said Impy, 'I promise.'

Chapter Fourteen

Baker Street

Found: *one briefcase, one toy dog, one school bag and a jewelled bird pendant on a chain with a broken catch*

When Edie arrived back she made a pot of tea for everyone and took a mug up the narrow stairs to Vera Creech. She paused in the doorway as the crow that occasionally sat on the windowsill had come inside and was perched on Vera's shoulder. Edie watched as Vera stretched her long delicate fingers to fish out a biscuit from a packet on her desk and broke off a half-moon shape. The crow pecked at the crumbs hungrily.

Edie tapped on the door to announce herself.

Vera turned quickly and the crow ruffled its feathers

and hopped onto Vera's arm. 'Edie! You shouldn't creep up on me like that.'

Edie put the mug on the desk. 'Can I feed it?'

'You can if you're careful,' Vera said, taking a sip of tea and pushing the packet towards her. 'I see you're back from your errand?'

'Yes, it didn't take long.' Edie picked up a digestive biscuit and broke it into pieces.

The crow cocked its head and looked at her out of the corner of its eye. Then it jabbed at the biscuit like a drill hammer.

'Why is he so tame?'

'I found him near Shadwell Station in East London underneath a railway arch. His wing was damaged.' Vera stroked his head with her long fingers. 'He's better now, though. I call him Shadwell because of where I found him.'

Shadwell jabbed again at the biscuit.

'I think I saw him down by Baker Street Station,' Edie said.

'There's a lot of crows in London, Edie,' said Vera. 'It probably wasn't him.'

Edie stretched out her other hand so that she too could pet the bird. She let her fingers slide over the sleek, oily feathers.

'Be careful,' warned Vera. 'He bites!'

At this Shadwell twisted his head round and nipped Edie's fingers hard. Then, snatching at the last of the biscuit, he hopped back through the open window and flew off into the branches of a London plane tree. Edie hid her fingers in her pocket.

'Funny, isn't it? That "Bakerloo Line" box has gone missing,' Vera said.

Edie felt cold. 'Gone missing?'

'Yes. Just disappeared apparently. I'll have to tell Ursula, of course.'

A buzzer sounded.

'That'll be your dad summoning us to the basement.'

They went down to help Dad with the last sacks of the day. Edie laid out a briefcase, a toy dog, a school bag and a jewelled silver bird pendant on a chain with a broken catch. Her fingers still smarted from the nip Shadwell had given her. Vera was busy jotting down all the items in her notebook that she would later transfer to Sherlock. Edie watched her neat hand.

Toy dog. White and fluffy. Found South Kensington.

School bag containing reading books (Beech Grove Primary School). Found Circle Line at Victoria.

When she got to the jewelled bird pendant she held it up but didn't seem to write anything down.

'What a pretty thing,' she said as if to herself, and twisted the catch to mend it.

'Right, time to go, Edie,' Dad said, folding the last of the sacks. 'Vera, can I leave you to lock up and put that pendant in the Cabinet of Valuables? Benedict's already left.'

'Of course, Mr Winter,' Vera said. She sat down at a table in the basement to finish her notes, still holding the bird pendant.

Edie fetched her coat and within minutes they were in the ticket hall at Baker Street Station. It was rush hour and people were crowding round the tops of the escalators. As they rode down, Edie took a sharp intake of breath. She thought she could see Vera Creech below them heading towards the tunnels. She was wearing a large overcoat and an odd little pillbox hat with a feather, but Edie felt sure she had glimpsed her streak of blue hair.

'Dad, didn't Vera Creech stay behind to lock up?'

'Yes. She often stays late.' He winked at Edie. 'I sometimes think she sleeps there!'

'But isn't that her down there – way ahead of us?'

They both looked down into the bustling crowds

below, but Vera (or her lookalike) was nowhere to be seen.

'Can't have been, Edie. She'd have had to sprout wings to get here first!' said Dad.

Chapter Fifteen

Alexandra Park Road

'Impy!' said Edie. 'You promised.'

Nid was missing.

Impy was standing in the pool of light cast by the desk lamp and Edie could hear Dad clattering pans downstairs as he prepared dinner.

'He must have slipped under the door.'

'Where do you think he's gone?' asked Edie.

'Probably looking for small shiny objects. Or eating Rice Krispies.'

'We'll have to find him.'

She emptied out her jar of hair clips that was sitting on her desk. Then she looked in her drawer among her paper clips and drawing pins.

'Let's try the Rice Krispies,' Edie said and ran down to the kitchen with Impy lodged in her plait and tipped the last of the Rice Krispies into a bowl. Nid was nowhere to be seen.

'Edie, you can't eat breakfast now,' said Dad. 'We'll be having dinner soon.'

'I-it's a science project,' said Edie quickly. 'I have to . . . er . . . find out why Rice Krispies go snap, crackle and pop.'

She pressed her ear to the bowl of cereal and tried to look as if she was undertaking a serious scientific experiment. It was a stupid excuse, but Dad was easily convinced.

'I think you might need milk,' he suggested.

At that moment the dog flap burst open and Bilbo shot inside as if he had been stung by a bee. Bilbo had a woolly coat like a sheep and his fluffy topknot looked slightly askew as he galloped through the kitchen and down the corridor towards the front door.

'Those squirrels must be up to no good,' said Dad, who was busy frying sausages. Edie guessed it wasn't the squirrels bothering Bilbo. She had distinctly heard a high-pitched cry of 'Yee-hah!' as Bilbo went past.

Within seconds Bilbo had skidded into a U-turn and come clattering back down the corridor. Edie grabbed him by the collar and spotted Nid sitting right in the centre of Bilbo's topknot. He was clutching two tufts of hair as if they were the reins of a rodeo horse, and he looked wild with excitement.

'Nid!' shouted Impy.

'Yee-hah!' said Nid again, and he pulled at the tufts of hair in an effort to goad Bilbo into another buffalo chase. Instead Bilbo sat down and began to scratch furiously at his ear and Nid's face turned to alarm as Bilbo stood up again and started to shake himself.

'Something's bothering him,' said Dad. Luckily one sausage started popping with hot grease and he turned his attention back to the pan.

Edie bent down and snatched Nid from Bilbo's top-knot and put him on the table. Still flushed with the excitement of his rodeo ride, he jumped into the sugar bowl.

Impy flitted down and stood in front of the bowl. 'You idiot,' she hissed. 'Why did you run off?'

Nid ignored her and was looking at the Rice Krispies packet. He performed a double somersault off the edge of the bowl, and, using a teaspoon as a lever, he sprang over the butter dish and landed upright at the bottom of the cereal box. Pushing his whole weight against it, he made it topple over, scattering crispy ovals of rice everywhere.

Dad swung round as they cascaded to the floor. 'Edie! Science project or not, this is too much. You'll have to clear the whole lot up.'

Nid darted about, picking up Rice Krispies, and then carried a pile of them back to the bowl, stacked up in his arms like a set of miniature pillows.

Dad handed Edie the dustpan and brush. 'Let me know when you're done.'

He carried a plate of sausages, toast and beans down the corridor to the sitting room and Edie heard the TV spring into life. Bilbo gave a small 'hrrmmph' and followed him.

Edie knelt down and swept up the remaining Rice Krispies. Nid was not going to be an easy guest.

'I'll help you,' said Impy, and she crawled under the kitchen units to pick up all the Rice Krispies and a few odd buttons that had scattered under there in among the sticky dust and clumps of dog hair.

'Now you are both going back upstairs,' Edie said when they were finished.

She carried Nid back up to the box with Impy whirring alongside.

'But we have to go and look for Jot!'

'We're not going anywhere tonight,' said Edie. 'Dad is already in a mood and you nearly got me into big trouble.'

'*Nid* nearly got you into trouble!' said Impy, scowling

at her younger brother.

Speckle appeared on the rim of the box clutching the walnut. He hadn't yet come out.

'I don't even know what Jot looks like,' Edie went on.

'He looks like Speckle!'

Speckle jumped back down into the box and reappeared almost immediately clutching a bottle top. It was a flattened silver one with a zigzag line of teeth round the edge. He held it out to Edie. She turned it over and saw that a picture had been painted on the inside of it in tiny vivid brushstrokes of colour. It showed two figures with the same tuft of hair; their arms were folded round one another's shoulders.

'It's a picture of Speckle and Jot,' said Impy. 'Speckle painted it. That's him on the left . . . and Jot is on the right.'

Edie was stunned by the detail. She could see the fingers on their hands, the strands of hair, the stitches on their bright blue tops and the line of their mouths, open in laughter.

'It's brilliant, Speckle,' she said.

Speckle nodded vigorously. Then he stared at Edie as if he were willing her to do something.

'Can you talk, Speckle?' Edie asked gently.

He shook his head.

'He writes messages and paints pictures instead,' Impy said.

'Why didn't Speckle go with Jot?'

'Just because they're twins it doesn't mean they're the same,' Impy said. 'Speckle likes to stay at home making things or looking after the nut, whereas Jot likes adventures. He'd roam around the edges of the Hillside Camp and chase spiders up the bank. And he'd go out at night with his friends in the tunnels around Highgate Station.'

Speckle had pulled out a small notebook from his bag and was writing something down. He pushed it towards Edie.

'*I 'fraid of the dark*,' she read. '*They call me scaredy-flit!*' Beside it was a drawing of a small frightened face.

'Jot's friends *did* call him that,' Impy said, placing her arm round Speckle's shoulder. 'And Jot fought them because of it.'

Edie looked again at the bottle top. She could see now that the twins *were* different, but she could also see that it mattered to Speckle more than anyone that Jot was missing.

'We'll go first thing tomorrow,' she said gently, returning the bottle top to him.

*

Impy nudged Nid and the three flits lined up in a row. Impy held out a small cloth bag to Edie. Using her finger and thumb, Edie took the bag and tipped the contents into the palm of her hand. There was a small silver windmill, a mother-of-pearl button and a single band of gold.

'Are they for me?' she asked.

Impy nodded vigorously.

'Did you find these in the house?'

'Yes,' said Impy. 'F7 work. The windmill and the button were underneath the floorboards and Nid found the ring at the back of the sink.'

'Can I keep this?' Nid asked, producing a broken ruler from behind his back. 'It's perfect for a skateboard ramp.'

'Yes,' said Edie, laughing.

*

Dad had fallen asleep in front of the television, so Edie gently shook him awake.

'Look what I've found, Dad.'

He sat up, rubbing his eyes.

'Have you cleared up those Rice Krispies?'

'Yes . . . and look.' She unfurled her hand and stood the windmill charm upright.

Dad stared at the cluster of objects. 'Ha! That windmill charm was something we brought back from a holiday in Amsterdam. I wondered where it had gone.' Then he gave a small gasp. 'That ring . . . well, that's your mum's wedding ring. It's been missing for years. Where did you find these?' He placed the ring in the palm of his hand.

'I-I found them when I was sweeping up,' said Edie, flushing slightly.

'Well, maybe it was a good thing that all those Rice Krispies spilled everywhere. Heta will be so pleased.'

Edie sat down beside him to eat her food.

'It's the milk that makes the Rice Krispies go snap, crackle, pop,' Dad said.

Later, back in her bedroom, Edie looked inside the box. Impy was swinging in the hammock and Nid was dipping his hand into the chocolate spread.

'Thanks,' said Edie. 'Tomorrow we'll go and look for Jot.'

Nid looked up and raised one sticky thumb in a tiny thumbs-up salute.

Chapter Sixteen

Alexandra Park Road to **High Barnet**

First thing next day, Dad had already left for work.

Edie stayed at home, telling Dad that she had other plans and was going to spend the day with some 'new friends', which seemed to please him. She began to organise the search party. Each flit carried a bag with all sorts of practical tools like pins, torches and tweezers, but there was a dispute over a thimble of sugar sprinkles.

'*I'm* carrying it!' said Impy.

'No, I am!' said Nid.

'Why do we need the sprinkles anyway?' said Edie.

'To lay a trail for Jot. He loves sugar. All flits do.'

Impy snatched the jar from Nid and stuffed it in her bag. Nid scooped up some loose sugar sprinkles and threw them at Impy, then he ran under the bed and reappeared rolling half a packet of Polos that he must have found in Edie's school bag. He levered one of the mints out, holding it in his arms as if it were a flit-sized rubber ring.

'You can't take that,' said Impy.

'It's OK,' said Edie, holding up both her hands. If she put Nid and the Polo in her pocket, it might keep him out of mischief. The dog flap clattered open downstairs as Bilbo set off on a squirrel patrol round the garden. Nid paused, looking towards the open door.

'No, Nid!' said Edie. She did *not* want a rerun of yesterday. 'If you come with us today, you have to stay in my sight!'

'Remember our cousins,' said Impy with a theatrical flourish.

She told Edie how Cousins Smidgen and Sprint had been stamped on during a particularly crowded rush hour and deaf old Uncle Wilmott had had a nasty accident in some train doors as they slid shut. Edie tried to imagine herself as flit-sized: ducking out of the way of bags and rucksacks, umbrellas and feet – *so many* smelly feet. Or, even worse, being sat on by a Londoner's giant bottom. No wonder Smidgen and Sprint hadn't survived.

Edie opened up her school planner and unfolded a map of the Underground, smoothing it down on her desk. 'Dad told me there's two hundred and fifty miles of track down there,' said Edie. They looked at the coloured lines as they crossed and circled round London like strands of spaghetti.

'First stop is the station near Charlie's house. That's where Jot said he would meet you. Can you remember where it was?'

Speckle eased himself out of the box for the first time and jumped down onto the map. He pointed at the marker for King's Cross Station and ran his finger from there along the Northern Line to the very top of the map. His finger came to rest at High Barnet.

*

A forest of legs filled the huge ticket hall at King's Cross. Shoes and boots clicked across the concourse, crossing this way and that as they headed for the barriers, and the air smelt of sweat and warm socks. It was hard not to think of Cousins Smidgen and Sprint.

Edie leant against the wall, checking that Nid and Speckle were still safely in her pocket. The floor was grimy and balls of dust and hair blew across it like tumbleweed. She pictured Jot alone, cowering in the shadows among the discarded takeaway boxes and old stubs of chewing gum, trying to navigate the busy platforms. She imagined the rush of warm air as the train came in, sucking at his arms and legs and wings, and clickety-click, clickety-click, pulling at him, trying to drag him into the windy blast.

The Northern Line train left the tunnel and travelled overground. They were in the suburbs of London, sandwiched between the inner city and the huge motorway that circled it like a ring doughnut. Edie looked out at the long back gardens either side of the tracks dotted with clumps of greenery and beyond them a sea of red-roofed houses. Metal footbridges crossed the line at every station and brambles grew along the fence. They started to climb uphill.

'Can you see Charlie's house from the station?' Edie asked. She suddenly felt overcome by the need to share the secret of the flits with someone else.

'Can we go there first . . . just to have a look?'

The train slid to a halt and Impy flew ahead up a pathway that led out of the station. It turned away from a busy high road and ran alongside a row of terraced houses. Charlie's house was the first one. It was nicely shabby, Edie thought, with sash windows at the front and pots of geraniums beside the door. The path ran alongside the back garden.

Impy pointed through the shrubbery at a large green shed with cobwebs across the window. An old skateboard was leaning against the front and pinned over the door was a basketball hoop. 'That's Charlie's shed,' she whispered.

'And Charlie's bedroom is up there,' said Nid, pointing

up to the back of the house, but there were no lights on.

'We should go,' said Impy, hovering in front of Edie. She looked anxious and Edie imagined the shed clearance and bag of 'jumble' might be weighing on her mind.

Edie turned back reluctantly and saw a boy coming up the path from the station wheeling a bicycle. She could tell straight away from the spiked hair that it was the boy she had seen on the Tube – Charlie's older brother Ivan. He was plugged into some earbuds and holding his phone. As he drew level with the house Edie knew she had to say something.

'Um, sorry . . . can I just ask you . . .?'

She felt Impy withdraw into the twists of her plait. Ivan looked up and pulled one of his earbuds out. He looked at her warily. 'Yeah?'

'Is Charlie in?'

'Um . . . no. He's away for a few days. Scouts or something.'

Edie felt crushed. She stood there, not sure what to say next. Charlie didn't even know who she was.

Nid scrabbled up her jacket and stood on her shoulder. 'You forgot us!' he shouted at the boy.

'Nid!' Edie whispered. Impy was sliding down her plait and in seconds she had grabbed hold of Nid's top and pulled him back into the shadows of Edie's neckline.

Ivan was looking at her blankly. 'Do you want me

91

to tell him you called by?' It was clear he hadn't seen or heard anything.

'No. It's all right, thanks.' Edie turned and raced back down the path with the flits.

They carefully searched the station for any sign of Jot, looking along the walls, in among the flower planters and under the benches.

'Nothing,' said Impy.

Nid was distracted by a crisp packet blowing along the platform and he ran after it, dabbing his finger in the salty crumbs that had stuck to the sides, but Speckle had been studying a patch of wall just past the waiting room. He put two fingers in his mouth and whistled. About a metre off the ground there were three pencilled letters of wobbly handwriting.

Jot

A small, crudely drawn arrow beneath Jot's name pointed to a crack in the wall and a corner of folded paper that was wedged there. Speckle eased it out and unfolded it and they all crowded round. Impy read aloud what he had written in tiny scratched lettering.

To my fambly,
I could not find u here even tho' I looked for a
long time. I know where Flum and the nut is,
but have gone to find help. Look out for magpins

and the spy bird. They are everywhere.
Your brother Jot

Speckle kicked at the paper and wiped away an angry tear.

'Why didn't he wait?' said Impy. 'Jot's so impatient.'

'We'll come back tomorrow and the next day,' said Edie. 'And let's leave something to tell him we've got his message.'

Nid had already climbed up the brickwork and, taking the silver thimble from his bag, he filled it with sugar sprinkles and placed it in the gap. Then as an afterthought he stuffed a Polo mint alongside it. Impy wrote a message on the back of a chocolate wrapper – *We are all safe. Will come back soon* – and Speckle threw Nid the bottle-top painting of the twin brothers. Nid stuck the bottle top to the wall just above Jot's name with a tiny stub of chewing gum.

Impy had moved away to study a Tube map further up the wall. 'Where to now?' asked Edie.

'Could we go to Highgate?' Impy called back. 'It's only six stations south of here.'

Speckle shook his head vigorously to say no.

'We should go, Speckle,' said Impy.

'Why?' asked Edie.

'You'll see,' said Impy.

Chapter Seventeen

High Barnet to **Highgate**

Edie held her hands cupped together in the ticket hall at Highgate Tube Station. She could feel Impy's breath as the flit peeped through her fingers. There were only a few passengers about.

'Where next?' whispered Edie.

'There's an old station above this one,' said Impy. 'You can get to it through a gap in the hedge across the car park.'

Edie climbed the steep staircase that led out of the ticket hall, and, as soon as they reached daylight, Impy eased Edie's fingers apart and fluttered off across the tarmac.

Edie waited until the passengers thinned out and there was no one about and then hurried after her, past a row of parked cars and through the gap in the hedge. There was a sign saying *No Entrance* and beyond it a path wound upwards between overgrown brambles and bushes. Edie edged around the sign and up the pathway, ignoring the thorns that caught in her hair and snagged at her ankles.

She reached a clearing and a set of concrete steps. Climbing the steps, she found herself standing on the platform of a disused station that led straight into a hillside.

The station was hidden from the car park by a tangle of plants that had sprung up right along the line of the fence. Stinging nettles curled themselves round the edges of the platform and moss covered the walls like old patchwork. Brittle autumn leaves blew this way and that, piling up against the old station buildings and

catching in the metal shutters of the ticket office. It looked deserted and unloved, but to Edie it was magical. A railway wilderness.

There was no sign of Impy.

Edie put her hand in her pocket and lifted out Nid and Speckle. Nid stood up, looked around him and did a series of excited star jumps on the palm of her hand, but Speckle crouched down and hid behind the ball of her thumb.

'What is this place?' Edie asked.

'It's our home,' said Nid.

It was so much bigger than she had imagined and so quiet and peaceful. A hidden corner of London that lay over Highgate Underground Station like a secret cloak. The distant rumble under her feet told her that the Tube trains ran deep below.

'The Hillside Camp?'

'Yes. The Camp's just up there,' said Nid, pointing up beyond the platform. 'But the spy bird found it and gave us away.'

'The spy bird?' said Edie.

'The crow.'

Edie thought about Shadwell, the tame crow with the nipping beak that sat on Vera's windowsill, but, as Vera had said, there were a lot of crows in London.

Edie looked up towards the hillside. The two tunnel

entrances that had once carried trains through it were boarded up. She walked to the end of the platform and jumped down. Nature had completely taken over. Brambles snaked this way and that and tree roots were sticking out of the ground where the train tracks would have run. She could smell rotting wood and wild thyme.

Nid dropped down into the long stalks of autumn grass and sprinted off and Edie tried to keep up with him as he darted through the undergrowth. She could hear Impy calling above her. 'Jo-ot? Flu-uum?'

A bat, soft and mouse-like, skimmed past Edie's ear. It startled her. Speckle slithered down her arm and back into her pocket.

'Impy?' Edie called out.

'Up here,' said a small choked voice.

Impy was sitting to one side of the tunnel entrance halfway up a bank. Tears dripped down her nose. 'There's nothing left,' she said.

Edie followed her gaze and saw amid the undergrowth rows of terraces like small streets cut into the side of the bank. Tiny houses that were built from the discarded rubbish of city life. Many were damaged. Wooden lollipop-stick planks were tossed about, tin-can walls buckled and bent, and an egg-box roof was crumpled and broken. Tiny cooking pots were turned over, chairs and tables scattered, beds unmade. The place was deserted.

Nid ran along one of the terraces and stopped at one of the houses. Outside it *Number 9* was painted in spidery writing. 'This was our house,' he said.

'Flu-uum? Jot?' cried Impy, jumping up and running after him. 'Is there anyone there?'

Her tiny cries echoed around the old station, bouncing off the brickwork round the old tunnels.

There was no reply.

Chapter Eighteen

High Barnet

For the next two days Edie and the flits travelled back to High Barnet, checking to see if Jot had returned, but the thimble of sugar sprinkles remained untouched and there were no more messages.

While Dad was at work they went further into town, searching Underground stations for Jot's name. At Brixton Station Speckle found a graffiti tag with *Aidan loves Bea* scratched inside a love heart. At Highbury Edie found three *Arsenals* written in large red letters and Nid found *Fuzz Bear* scrawled in thick black felt-tip behind a bench in Moorgate, but there weren't any tags like Jot's.

Impy flew into numerous tunnels calling into the darkness. 'Jot! Jo-ot!'

She would emerge minutes later, buffeted and grimy from the passing trains. She had said very little since they had left the deserted camp. All her energy and fizz had disappeared.

There were more and more reports of valuables disappearing on the Underground. Passengers described leaving home wearing valuable items and how they had magically disappeared, unfelt and unseen. The papers spoke of pickpockets so light-fingered and deft that they must have had powers of invisibility. Strange birds appeared too, flapping out of tunnels, perching on escalators and pecking at people's hats. Edie immediately thought that these could be magpins seizing anything that was shiny. The Lost Property Office now was inundated with enquiries.

Edie tried to tell Dad that maybe it was birds that were stealing things, but he dismissed the idea as a flight of fancy.

*

Sunday was the last day before half-term ended, and Dad was going to spend the afternoon at the Lost Property Office with Benedict as he was working overtime to respond to all the reports of missing items.

'Meet me there at five p.m. and we'll go for a fish-and-chip supper on Lisson Grove,' he said.

That meant there would be time for one last search

for Jot. At about four o'clock Edie and the flits stopped for a snack on a bench at the far end of the platform at Russell Square. The flits sat in a circle on Edie's rucksack nibbling at a digestive biscuit.

There was a lull in the trains and passengers were beginning to congregate. A woman came to sit beside Edie and after a few minutes she closed her eyes with her hands resting on her lap. Edie noticed that she was wearing rings on her left hand. One was gold with a red stone and another had a spray of small flowers picked out in tiny chips of diamond. They looked expensive. The woman dozed fitfully and Edie was eating a biscuit when a sudden movement caught her eye. A small creature was creeping up onto the back of the woman's hand.

'Impy,' whispered Edie, 'look!'

The creature looked to Edie like a very young flit. It was smaller even than Nid and its hair looked soft and fluffy, but it was dressed in rough clothes and had bare feet. It reached the woman's finger and with tiny deft hands it began to ease one of the rings off. Impy flew upwards and hovered over the flit just as it was slipping the ring round its waist like a gym hoop.

'What are you doing?' she demanded.

The tiny flit stared up at her and then ran back across the woman's lap. Impy followed it, leaning downwards to tug at the ring.

'You can't take that,' she said. 'Don't you *know* your Ten Forager Don't Ever Dos?'

The flit said nothing and struggled with the hoop.

Impy tugged too and bombarded it with questions. 'Who are you? Where are you from?'

This time the flit turned and bit her on the hand to make her let go, and then scrabbled along the bench and down to the floor.

'Ow!' said Impy, nursing her hand.

It ran fast, bobbing along the seam of the wall in among the dust and hair balls. Up ahead of it Edie spotted a thin gold chain snaking along the floor.

'There's more of them!' Nid cried, and somersaulted off the bench after them. The small flits ran faster, even with the chain bumping along behind them, but Nid was quick. He had almost caught them when a magpin hopped out from behind a bin. It had been waiting for them. It lowered its wing and the flit thieves scrabbled up it and clung onto its neck feathers. It turned and flew like a dart over the heads of the waiting passengers and into the tunnel. The gold chain streamed out like a banner behind them.

'Did you *see* that?' said Edie. 'They're working together.'

At that moment the train came in and the woman woke up and leapt up to catch it.

Edie didn't dare call out to the woman. If she rang the police and they discovered her dad worked at the Lost Property Office it would only make everything worse. No one would believe her. She could only watch as the Tube-train doors slid shut behind her. It wouldn't be long before the woman looked down at her hands and realised that her ring was missing.

Chapter Nineteen

Baker Street

Dad and Benedict were alone when Edie arrived at the Lost Property Office. They were going through the Cabinet of Valuables, trying to match up dozens of enquiries to the items they had actually found.

Edie went to the first floor to make them tea. As she waited for the kettle to boil she looked up the stairs towards Vera's office, but it was in darkness. She left the flits playing football with a paper-clip goal and a dried pea and went upstairs. There was something she wanted to check. Switching on the light, she picked up Vera's notebook, and ran her finger down the entries for Tuesday 26 October. She found the toy dog and the school bag, but nothing about any jewelled bird pendant.

As she turned to leave, she heard a clatter from one of the drawers. Edie eased the top one open. Inside were two sharpened pencils, a bowl filled with sugar lumps and a fluffy sock. Laid out on a small handkerchief beside the sock were the inner workings of a watch, cogs and wheels and tiny screws all set out in a row beside the glass clockface as if someone was in the middle of a repair.

A sugar cube toppled out of the bowl and Edie saw what looked like a small head duck down among the other cubes. She stared at the bowl and the seconds ticked past. Then up it popped again, a very round head with a frizz of hair. It was a flit, Edie was convinced of it. It dropped out of sight again.

'Jot,' she whispered. 'Is that you?'

She gently lifted the bowl out onto the desk and knelt down until her eyes were level with it. She picked up the fallen lump of sugar and held it over the bowl, and within seconds a tiny hand stretched up and took it.

'Impy,' she called down the stairs. 'Come up here. Quick.'

In seconds Impy was hovering beside her, followed by Nid and Speckle. Edie pointed at the sugar bowl and mouthed, 'Jot!'

105

Impy dived in, pulling at the sugar lumps until they revealed a rather round-faced flit, looking very alarmed. He was nothing like Impy or Speckle or the bottle-top painting. He clambered up out of the bowl and tried to run across the desk, but his body was plump and his legs very short. Every time he stumbled, he bounced back up again like a miniature ping-pong ball.

Impy grabbed him by the ankles and wrestled him to the ground. 'Who are you?' she said, standing over him.

'I'm Bead. B-b-but I don't know anything,' said the flit in a way that suggested he possibly did. He wriggled about. 'Let me GO!'

Nid pulled some sugar strands out of his bag and pushed towards him. Bead looked at them adoringly.

'You can have them all if you tell us more,' said Nid.

Bead stretched out his fingers and grasped a handful.

'Did the magpins attack your camp?'

'Attack?' said Bead, filling his mouth with the sweet sugar strands. 'No. I ran away from my home camp. It's not in London, but further down the Thames near Tilbury. I wanted to come to the city.'

'What are you doing in here?' said Edie.

'I work for Miss Creech. She found me at Marylebone Station. She was eating chips and I was trying to take one.'

'What do you do for her?'

Bead turned pink in the face. 'She feeds me and I fix

things. Like old watches.' He waved at the cogs and wheels lying in the drawer. Even Edie could tell he wasn't telling the whole truth.

'Do you know anything about young newly hatched flits that are missing?' Impy said.

Bead didn't answer this. Instead, with one final wriggle, he pulled his feet free and, scooping up more sugar strands, he jumped back into the drawer. 'Go away!' he shouted, crawling into his sock.

Edie bent down towards the drawer. She had one burning question that she needed to ask. 'But how can Miss Creech *see* you?'

There was a pause. 'She's got an eyeglass,' Bead said from deep inside the sock . 'It was because of me that she realised she could see us. She was looking through the eyeglass, trying to work out what it was, when I crept up to steal her chips.'

'Where is it?' Impy demanded of the sock.

'Don't know!' came the muffled reply.

'I've seen it!' said Edie. 'She wears it round her neck.'

'It's all wrong, Bead,' Impy called out to the sock. 'She shouldn't be able to see you. Does she wear it all the time?'

'No.' Bead stuck his head out of the sock. 'I guard it for her sometimes.' He stood up, eyeing them all. 'I'll show it to you . . . for a price, of course!'

Edie dipped her hand into her pocket and fished out

the last of a packet that contained two fruit gums. She had kept them in reserve for Nid. She held out a green one.

'Both,' said Bead.

He drives a hard bargain, thought Edie, as she dropped both into the drawer beside him.

Bead disappeared into the back of the drawer and returned dragging a pouch that had a shape tooled into its leather. The outline of a tiny figure running.

Impy jumped into the drawer beside Bead.

'Where did Vera get it from?' she asked.

'She found it,' said Bead.

'Where?' If Vera had found it on an Underground train or a London bus, then why hadn't she reported it to the Lost Property Office?

'I don't know,' said Bead, looking at his feet.

Edie took the leather pouch and pulled out the eyeglass. She let the chain dangle through her fingers and held the glass disc up to her face. Everything seemed so horribly magnified that it made her feel a little sick. She could see every detail on the wheels and watch cogs, and Impy's face was weird and distorted. There was a soft beating against the window that made Edie look up. Feathers filled the eyeglass and Shadwell swam into view on his perch on the sill outside. His ringed eye looked huge and cold like a marble.

'It's the spy bird,' whispered Impy. 'We should go.'

'Shadwell is a spy bird?' said Edie, dropping the eyeglass.

'Yes, I'm sure of it,' said Impy. 'Spy birds watch you and once they've seen you they never forget. It was probably a spy bird that found all our flit camps.'

Edie flung open the window. 'I know what you are! And Vera is up to something too! Shoo! Go away!'

The crow turned its back on her and, flapping its wings, it lifted up into the evening sky.

Bead jumped back into the safety of his sock. 'Oh dear. Oh dear! I don't think you should have done that. Quick. Give me back the eyeglass. When Shadwell comes it usually means Miss Creech is on her way. You should go!'

Edie could hear the clank of the lift coming up to the first floor below.

She slipped the eyeglass back in its pouch and closed Bead's drawer with Bead inside, then she gathered up the flits and hurried back down the stairs.

'Hide!' she said. The flits scattered: Nid and Speckle into Edie's coat and Impy into the teapot. Edie stood by the kettle trying to look busy.

The lift door opened and Benedict appeared in the doorway. Edie felt as if she might faint with relief.

'I was just coming up to see if you were all right, Edie. It's been a while. The tea?'

'I'm just doing it now,' said Edie, putting teabags into two mugs.

'Right,' said Benedict. 'Well, maybe we should forget the tea, Edie. We're almost done downstairs. Your dad's keen to take us all off for fish and chips. Get your coat and we'll go.' He turned and went back downstairs.

'It was only Benedict,' Edie said, turning back to the teapot.

Impy's head popped out of the spout but she peeped round past Edie and then shot up her sleeve.

'Who were you talking to?' a voice said behind her. Edie froze. She turned slowly round. Vera was standing at the bottom of her office stairs. The eyeglass was now dangling round her neck.

'No one. I mean, myself. I was just talking to myself. I-I didn't see you come in.'

Vera removed her coat and hat. She lifted the eyeglass to her face and was walking around the room, digging in pencil pots and tipping up the mugs on the drainer. She stopped right in front of Edie, so close that the feather of her pillbox hat tickled her. 'I hope you weren't snooping, Edie,' she said. Her right eye looked enormous through the eyeglass.

'N-no. Just finishing up here.' Edie moved to one

side and grabbed her coat. She could feel Vera's breath on her neck. 'I-I should go. Dad's waiting.'

'Well, I mustn't keep you,' Vera said coolly. 'But I don't like snoops.' She turned round and walked back up the stairs to her office.

Edie dragged on her coat with the flits inside and hurried back downstairs to Dad and Benedict.

'You look as if you've seen a ghost, Edie,' Dad said.

'Vera gave me a fright, that's all – coming in suddenly like that.'

'Vera?' said Dad. 'She's not in today.'

'She was just upstairs,' said Edie.

'Can't be. We'd have seen her come in.'

'She's up there now. I just *saw* her, Dad.'

Benedict went off to check, but it wasn't long before he was back.

'All the lights are out up there. No one's in her office. Odd, though, that I found the fire escape on the latch.'

'And why would she be lurking about and leaving by the fire escape?' said Dad.

Edie decided not to protest any more, as she didn't want anyone to know that she'd been in Vera's office, but it *did* seem odd. She peered into the Cabinet of Valuables, trying to find the jewelled bird pendant, but, as far as she could see, it wasn't there.

Chapter Twenty

Alexandra Park Road

That night, on a Skype call to Finland, Edie asked her mum when she would be coming home.

'I miss you, Mum.'

'I miss you too, Edie, so much, but it'll only be a few more days.'

'Is it cold there?' Edie asked.

'It is. You can see your breath, and they say it's going to snow soon.'

As they talked, groups of children ran excitedly past the window of Edie's house dressed as witches and ghouls for Halloween.

'Have you been out trick or treating?' Mum asked.

'No. Dad and I set out the pumpkin, though. It's on the gatepost.'

'I thought you'd go out with Naz and Linny like last year.'

Edie tried not to think of her primary-school friends at a Halloween party, dressing up and painting each other's faces chalk white and blood red, and screaming with excitement in the cold autumn air.

'Didn't want to,' she said.

Mum looked surprised but said nothing.

'Mum?'

'Yes.'

'When you were little, did you believe in magic or strange creatures? Like mice that talked or elves or pixies?'

'Well, Granny Agata believed in house elves and she used to tell me stories about them. Finnish people call them *kotitonttu*. They used to help her keep the house tidy – or so she said – and make her potatoes grow and mend her broken china.'

'Like Dobby in *Harry Potter*?' asked Edie.

Mum laughed. 'Yes, a bit like Dobby, I suppose, but you never see them.'

'Never. Not even a tiny glimpse?'

'Well, I never did,' said Mum. 'But Granny Agata assured me they were there.'

'Maybe you've just forgotten, Mum?'

After they finished Skyping there was a knock on the door. Edie went into the hallway to pick up a bowl of

Halloween sweets and opened the door to a coven of witches. It was Naz and Linny and two other girls from school wearing black cobweb dresses and pointed hats. Linny's hair was braided with fluorescent beads. She gave a horrible cackle and waved a hand of green fingernails in Edie's face. 'Snakes' tongues and frogs' legs!' she shrieked.

Edie stood in silence, feeling horribly dull and left out in her plain clothes and slippers.

'Do goblins live here?!' shouted an older girl, who was wearing a skeleton suit and standing at the gate. All the witches cackled with laughter.

Edie offered the bowl to the witches and Linny peered into it.

'Is that all you got?' she said in a very unwitchlike voice. 'Bit babyish, isn't it?'

Edie looked at the jelly beans and dolly mixtures that Dad had shaken into the bowl earlier. Linny sniffed but grabbed a large handful, stuffing it into her already-overflowing plastic witch's cauldron. Then she ran screaming and shrieking down the garden path after the two other girls, but Naz lingered for a second.

'Too babyish for you too?' asked Edie.

It came out. She had spoken to Naz, even though it was a harsh thing to say. Why should she care about them any more? She had her own tribe to think about now.

Naz didn't take anything from the bowl, but she

pressed something into Edie's hand and ran down the path after the others. It was a beautiful chocolate spider wrapped in green-and-silver paper with six hairy legs.

Chapter
Twenty-One

Alexandra Park Road

The next evening, the bell rang and Edie opened the door to find Ada clutching a bag of cooking equipment in one hand and Baby Sol in the other. Her heart sank.

'I'm babysitting tonight,' said Ada. 'Hope you don't mind me bringing him along.'

Behind Ada came Juniper dressed in a coat with a fake-fur collar.

'That baby is SO annoying,' Juniper said. 'Once it starts crying, it never stops.'

At this Baby Sol beamed and shouted, 'Daba-DAH!'

'No school today, Juniper?' Dad asked.

'Inset day,' said Juniper grandly as if it were, in fact, the queen's birthday and she had authorised it.

Juniper lived somewhere on the other side of the River Thames in South London. She was in the same school year as Edie, but she behaved as if she was two or three years older.

She held out her coat. 'Hang it up, please, Edie. I don't want it all squashed and creased.'

Ada and Dad clattered about in the kitchen as they prepared Ada's curry and Baby Sol lay on a cushion in Bilbo's basket, kicking his legs in the air. They talked about the latest spate of thieving that had now spread to Londoners' houses and even a jewellery shop. It was thought the pickpockets were sneaking in by climbing through the drains and air vents from the Underground tunnels below.

Edie chopped onions and Juniper announced that she was going to lay the table.

She bustled about as if she were preparing for a banquet, spreading the table with the Winters' best cloth and laying out three sets of cutlery. Edie wrestled with a half-moon of onion. As she chopped away, the raw slices made her eyes water. She thought of Impy upstairs, and was furious that Ada's plan to get her and Juniper together had meant that she and the flits couldn't carry on searching for Jot after school.

'Eee-die, I need some help!' Juniper called through to the kitchen.

Edie put down her knife. It was a relief to escape the onion at least.

'Can you make these?' said Juniper, demonstrating how to fold a paper napkin into a fussy rosette. As Edie struggled with the napkins, Juniper took Mum's Finnish glass candlesticks out of the cupboard and set them on the centre of the table.

'You can't use those. It's not Christmas!' Edie exploded.

'So what?' said Juniper. 'They look nice. Why use them once a year?'

'They belong to Mum,' said Edie. 'And they only *ever*

come out at Christmas!' She felt her voice rising at the wrongness of it all.

'So what?' said Juniper again. 'I'm the guest, so I should be allowed to choose.'

Edie snatched up one of the candlesticks. She longed for her mum to be there to back her up. Dad appeared in the doorway holding the pot of curry. He bridled slightly at the sight of the candlesticks.

'I just wanted to make the table look nice,' said Juniper in a voice coated with sugar. 'But Eee-die thinks I should put them away.'

Dad looked uncomfortable. He cleared his throat. 'Well, it is a special occasion, I suppose. And the table does look very nice, Juniper. Let's leave the candlesticks where they are.'

Edie felt her cheeks burn with fury as she poked her fork at the curry later. It was *not* a special occasion and Mum was miles away. How could Dad be such a traitor?

As they ate, Juniper talked almost non-stop. She told them about her speech and drama classes, her debating club and her Year Seven prize for French. 'Oh, and I must tell you about my cross-country running.' She opened up the photo gallery on her smartphone. 'Look, here's me. That's me *again*. And that's my medal.'

There were several close-up pictures of the medal. Ada beamed and Mr Winter nodded, although he raised his eyebrows at the medals and winked at Edie. Edie looked away.

'Did you go trick or treating?' Juniper asked Edie. 'I went dressed as the Witch of the East in silver shoes with pointed toes and an icicle broomstick and I got over a hundred sweets in my bucket. The best thing was a blood-red lollipop with a skeleton inside. What did *you* get?'

'I didn't get anything because I didn't go,' said Edie. 'Except a chocolate spider,' she added.

'That's weird. Haven't you got any friends?'

Edie looked at her plate. She felt speechless. Impy was her best friend now, but she wasn't the kind of friend that Juniper meant.

'What did you do with that cradle, Edie?' Ada suddenly asked. 'The miniature cradle from the shop with the little quilt?'

'I-I put it upstairs,' said Edie.

'I bet it looks pretty on a shelf somewhere. Can I see what you've done with it?'

Edie did *not* want Ada to come upstairs or to see the box.

'I'll get it for you – no need for you to come up; I'll just bring it down. My bedroom's a horrible mess,' she said in a rush.

Edie headed upstairs and slipped into her bedroom,

carefully shutting the door behind her. She eased the box out from under the bed and rested it on her lap.

Impy looked up as Edie peered in. 'Are you finished yet?'

'No,' said Edie, 'Juniper and her grandmother are still downstairs, and she used Mum's Christmas candlesticks and Mum isn't even here.' She felt better being able to tell Impy about her awful guest.

'Will they go soon?' asked Impy.

'Hope so. I just need to borrow the nut cradle for a few minutes.'

She gently lifted out the cradle and put it in her pocket. She wished that it had a real flit nut in it.

'What will you name the baby flit if he's a boy?' Edie asked.

'I feel sure it's a girl,' said Impy. 'But what if it's already hatched and the magpins . . .?'

The door opened and Juniper filled the doorway.

'I heard you talking to someone, Edie.' She looked about the room. 'Or were you talking to yourself?'

Edie snapped the lid of the box shut, straining to hear the lock click into place. For once Impy didn't complain. 'I-I was practising lines for a play we're doing in drama,' she said. It was a feeble excuse and she knew that the beady-eyed Juniper had seen Edie close the box.

'So what's this?' she asked, sitting down heavily on

the edge of the mattress. She dragged the box towards her so that it rested on her knee and peered in at the tiny panes of glass.

'Give it back, plea-zze,' said Edie. The words buzzed out of her mouth like an angry wasp.

'What's so special about it?' Juniper said.

They tussled with it, pulling it back and forth between them, until Juniper, who was a bit taller than Edie, stood up and lifted the box above Edie's head. As she did she somehow managed to press the button and the lid sprang open.

Juniper gave a small gasp. 'A box with a secret lock?'

Edie tried to snatch the box back, but Juniper held it up high above her head and ran out of the bedroom and down the corridor to the bathroom.

'Give it back, Juniper!' cried Edie, running after her, but Juniper was already inside the bathroom and locking the door.

Edie slumped against it. 'I just want to see what's inside,' Juniper said through the bathroom door. 'I'm your *guest*, remember?'

Edie pressed her eye against the keyhole and could see Juniper settling on the floor beside the bath and folding herself over the box.

'It's not yours,' she shouted, pummelling at the door with her fists. 'It belongs to the Lost Property Office.'

Juniper ignored her, so Edie knelt down and looked through the keyhole again. For a moment Juniper's brow furrowed as she focused on the contents of the box and there was a silence before Juniper screamed with delight.

'Fairies!' she cried. 'I knew you were hiding something, Edie Winter.'

She held the lid open and stared inside, her eyes widening. Edie felt sweat pricking at her forehead as she rested it against the bathroom door.

Impy flew up and stood on the edge of the bath directly in Juniper's eyeline. She stared at Juniper with her fiercest look.

'Hello, little fairy,' Juniper whispered. 'Are your clothes made of flower petals?'

'I am not a fairy!' Impy shouted back. 'I do NOT wear petals or flower cups. Yuck!'

Juniper held out her finger as if it were a perch for a small bird. 'I'm going to call you Blossom,' she said. 'Stand on my finger.'

Impy lifted off and whirred furiously round her head, her sweet-paper top glinting in the mirror.

'Please, Juniper, you have to give the box back to me,' Edie said through the door.

Juniper ignored this. Instead she watched Impy, laughing and snatching at her as she tried to catch her. 'Bloss-som. Little Bloss-som.'

Impy quickly became tired of ducking and diving and, wary of Juniper's hand, she landed back on the edge of the bath. Juniper's finger moved towards Impy again and formed a ledge just in front of her feet.

'Come on, Blossom,' she said.

'I'm not called Blossom!' yelled Impy.

Then she bent down and bit Juniper on the tip of her finger. As Juniper felt the sharp pinprick she pulled her hand back sharply.

'Ouch!' She sucked her finger thoughtfully.

'Juniper,' Ada called up the stairs, 'time to go-ho! Baby Sol has to go home.'

Edie could hear the baby starting to cry downstairs, but Juniper ignored Ada, and Edie could see her left hand quietly pulling her phone out of her pocket.

'Fly, Impy!' shouted Edie through the door. 'Don't keep still!'

Impy lifted off again, whirring up into the air, until she was nothing but a fuzzy line twisting and turning this way and that. Juniper pointed her phone, pressing the camera button as she snapped at the air.

'JUNIPER!' Ada called. 'I have to get the baby home. Bilbo sat on him by accident.'

Edie could tell from the wheezing and gasping that Ada was starting to climb the stairs. The wails of the baby grew louder so Juniper put her phone in her pocket and unlocked the bathroom door. Edie slumped to one side, exhausted, as all the fight went out of her. Nothing mattered now – Juniper knew Edie's secret.

Ada reached the top of the stairs. 'Ah, here you are,' she said, 'playing a lovely game, I expect. Where's that doll's cradle, Edie? You never showed it to me?'

Edie slowly stood up and pulled the cradle out of her pocket.

'Look at that,' said Ada. 'Such a pretty thing. Juniper, have you seen this?'

'I've seen everything I need to, Gran,' said Juniper, and she handed the box back to Edie. At the top of the stairs she gave Edie a fake hug. 'And Edie and I have made friends!'

She tapped her nose as if she were in a spy film. 'Our secret,' she whispered as she set off after Ada.

'I'll have a look in the shop for some other miniature things,' Ada called up to Edie, 'when I get back from my child-minding trip.'

Trip? What trip? thought Edie.

The door banged shut below her and the baby's wails slowly disappeared down the street.

'I never want to see that awful girl again,' Impy said. Then she flew into the box of her own accord and asked Edie to close the lid.

*

Later that evening, Edie switched on her phone and looked for Juniper's Instagram account. She found it easily under @JunipBerry and quickly scrolled through the endless cross-country running photos, and ones of Juniper posing in her stupid fake-fur coat.

Juniper's latest post pinged up. The caption read: *I saw a fairy today!!!*

Edie stared at the image, expecting to see Impy's tiny face furiously looking back at her out of the screen. She could see the bathroom, the cabinet on the wall and the corner of the bath, but the image showed nothing else except the tiniest hazy blur in the top corner.

'She missed you, Impy,' breathed Edie, and she smiled as someone else had commented: *Fairies don't Xist, @JunipBerry – think u might be seeing things.*

Chapter Twenty-Two

Alexandra Park Road

The next afternoon Edie arrived home late after trampolining at school to find the door open. Dad was drinking tea in the kitchen, and there was a scattering of cups and plates and a half-eaten packet of biscuits.

'Ada and Juniper dropped by earlier. Juniper said she had forgotten something.'

At that moment Edie knew. 'Juniper? Why did they come HERE? You didn't let her go upstairs, did you?'

Before Dad could say anything, Edie had propelled herself up the stairs three steps at a time and stumbled through the doorway of her bedroom. She stared at the empty space under her bed. The flit box had gone. Frantically Edie scrabbled around her room, calling out for Impy, Nid and Speckle. She looked around her room and shook out the curtains. After ten minutes she realised that they really had gone. She thumped back down the stairs ashen-faced.

'Where's Juniper gone?'

'Ada was taking Juniper back home to South London,' Dad said. 'Then she's off on a week's holiday somewhere to help Baby Sol's family. That can't be bad, can it? A spot of winter sun.' So that was what Ada had meant by 'her trip'.

'Was Juniper carrying a box?' Edie almost shouted.

'I don't know,' said Dad, looking confused. 'They had a couple of bags.'

'Did she go upstairs?' said Edie.

'Er . . . yes, I think she did. Just before they left, but only to go to the bathroom.'

Edie began to sob. 'She's taken it.'

'Taken what?'

Edie's face was mottled and tear-stained. She beat her fist on the table with a loud thump. 'My *box*.'

Dad became very still and Edie knew immediately that she had made a terrible mistake.

'What do you mean, *your* box?' he said quietly.

'The box from the Storeroom at the End,' Edie said in a small voice.

Dad's anger blew up like a squally wind. 'That should NOT have come home, Edie Winter.'

'I'm sorry,' she said, her voice now so thin she could

barely hear it. '*Dad, I'm sorry.*'

She ran back upstairs and searched her room again, longing to see Impy hovering above her or Nid's head pop up like a meerkat. She pulled everything out of her wardrobe, but the box wasn't there. Snatching up her phone, she checked and rechecked @JunipBerry's Instagram account, but there was nothing apart from a couple of new selfies.

The empty spaces seemed to stare back at her, accusing her of being stupid. She was supposed to be protecting Impy's family and helping them to find Jot and Flum. Vera Creech, the spy bird and the magpins were the threat, *not* Juniper, and yet it was Juniper who had spoilt everything.

*

Edie didn't go down for supper and Dad left her alone. She lay face down on the bed so that she couldn't see the empty space where the box had sat. She could hear the gush of the tap downstairs and the clink of plates as Dad tidied the kitchen. She wished that Mum was here; even if Mum hadn't believed in the flits, she would have understood that the box was special. Magical. She rolled over onto her back and stared at the ceiling.

'He-lpp! Eee-die?' cried a muffled voice.

Edie sat up and looked around the room. It was coming from her chest of drawers.

'He-lloo?' cried the voice again.

She jumped up and pulled open the drawers one by one. In the top-left drawer in among a tangle of school socks she found Nid.

'Ni-id!' she croaked. 'You're still here.'

She scooped him up in her hand and folded her thumb round him. He sat on it, blinking in the light, as Edie plied him with questions.

'How come you weren't taken? Did Juniper see you?'

'I wasn't in the box. I was looking at the fish,' he said, pointing at the guppy fish who were swimming back and forth across the tank.

'That girl . . . Joooniper . . . ran in and stole the box, snapping the lid shut. It was all so quick. I thought she would catch me too so I jumped into the sock drawer to hide and buried myself at the back. I was scared to come out and eventually I fell asleep. When I woke up the drawer was shut fast.'

So Nid had been there all along. Dad had been doing the laundry earlier and probably closed Edie's drawers.

Nid slumped forward. 'So she took the box? Impy would never have left Speckle. She must have got them both.'

'I know,' said Edie sadly.

Nid turned away from Edie and furiously wiped his eyes. 'Never been alone before,' he said, sniffing loudly.

'You're not alone,' said Edie. 'I'm going to help you find them. All of them.'

'OK,' he said in a small voice, then he stood up and did a small star jump. 'Right, what's the plan?'

'We'll go to Ada's shop tomorrow after school and try to find out where Juniper lives.' Edie's feelings of despair began to evaporate. She still had Nid to reassure her that the flits were real and had become part of her life. Nid leapt off the chest of drawers and, using the string of lights hanging from Edie's wardrobe, he abseiled to the floor. There was a light ping from the phone that was still lying on her bed. Edie grabbed it and swiped to @JunipBerry. Her heart skipped a beat. 'Look at this!' She crouched down beside Nid and showed him the Instagram post.

It was a picture of Speckle sitting on a plastic toadstool in a strange red outfit and pointed hat. He was eating an iced gem biscuit. Within seconds three of her followers had commented.

Weird!

Wow, he looks real. What's he made of?

So sweee-et! Little pixie boy.

Edie's fingers hovered over the keypad. She knew that it would be better to remain silent so that Juniper wouldn't know she was watching her Instagram account. She wouldn't actually post it, but she couldn't stop herself from tapping out: *U are a thief.*

Chapter Twenty-Three

Alexandra Park Road to **school**

It was the second lesson of the school day. Maths. Edie's class was studying geometry and Mr Binding had drawn a series of angles on the whiteboard. He pointed at each one, barking to the class, 'Acute or obtuse?'

She'd hated leaving Nid at home, but he'd agreed to stay in her room with the guppy fish for company and the sock drawer for a quick getaway. He had strict instructions not to bother Bilbo, and it *was* only for the morning.

Edie's attention strayed across to the window. A large rectangle of tarmac dotted with red bins stretched away from the classroom. In half an hour Year Seven would be ushered out there to stand around in the cold. At primary school they would have charged outside to the playground, arguing about which game they were going to play: Homey, Red Letter or It.

No one played those games here. Instead a few of the Year Sevens kicked a football about or lobbed basketballs through a broken net, but mostly they just huddled together in small knots, crowding round their phones and laughing. Edie couldn't understand why they laughed so much.

'Edie Winter, acute or obtuse?'

Mr Binding prodded at the whiteboard and Edie made a wild guess. 'Obtuse, sir?'

'Absolutely right. Well done.'

Linny, who was sitting a couple of rows in front of her, turned round and mouthed 'know-it-all' at her and nudged her friend.

'Right, 7E. Settle down now. Books open. Please construct an obtuse angle of one hundred and twenty degrees and an acute angle of thirty degrees using your geometry sets.'

Raphael put his hand up.

'I know what you're going to say, Raphael,' said Mr Binding. 'Yet again you've left your geometry set at home. You'll just have to improvise.'

'What's "improvise" mean, sir?' Raphael asked.

'It means "be creative with what you've got",' said Mr Binding.

Edie unzipped her bag and pulled out her geometry set. She lined up her protractor and then fished in her pencil case for her sharpest pencil. Something was catching at it, something jammed in the corner against her rubber. Peering in, she caught sight of two small feet and froze.

It was Nid, wedged behind her rubber and clutching a boiled sweet. Riding Bilbo was one thing, but finding his way into her school bag was much worse. There were thirty children in this class and they were all under thirteen.

She glared at Nid, unable to say anything. Then she scribbled *Don't Come Out* on a piece of paper and pushed it towards him. He ignored it and popped his head up through the zip of the pencil case like a periscope.

'So this is *school*!' he whispered. To her horror he wriggled through the gap and jumped down onto the desk.

'Edie Winter, get on with your work, please,' said Mr Binding from the front as he settled down to some marking. Everyone else was bent over their desks, except Raphael who was signalling to Conor. He held up a broken pencil, looking as if he might cry.

'Settle *down*, class!' said Mr Binding. 'Raphael! Do I have to say it again? Improvise!'

'But Mr Binding . . . ?'

'I don't want to hear another word.'

'He needs a sharpener,' whispered Nid. 'I'll get one for him.'

'No!' Edie whispered.

Edie snatched at him but he slipped out of her grasp, hopped up onto the windowsill and hid behind a pile of maths books. Edie half stood up and reached her hand behind the books, trying to grab him.

'Edie, sit down and GET ON!' said Mr Binding.

Edie sank back into her seat, her heart racing. With shaky hands she lined up the protractor again and started to draw an angle, watching the windowsill out of the corner of her eye. For a few minutes all was quiet.

The sill doubled up as a storage area for stationery. Maths books, boxes of pens and pads of paper were lined up along it and at the far end Edie could see a whole jar of metal pencil sharpeners. Nid had spotted them too.

It all happened very fast.

He set off somersaulting and cartwheeling towards the jar with his legs in a blur. Edie gave a tiny strangled gasp. She looked around the classroom. Every head was bent over their work apart from Raphael, who was trying to make his broken pencil work. Could Nid get there and back without *anyone* noticing? He landed neatly beside the jar and clambered up onto a pile of exercise books. He leant over and reached inside, easing one of the sharpeners upwards, but it slipped out of his grasp.

He leant further in and toppled forward slightly. The jar wobbled and then crashed to the floor, scattering pencil sharpeners.

Mr Binding's head snapped up. 'What was that?' he said.

Edie looked helplessly at Nid. He had grabbed a sharpener and was running back along the windowsill like a dried pea that had been fired out of a catapult. Linny and another girl who were sitting in the desks a couple of rows in front of Edie looked over at the window too.

'Aaaah!' screamed Linny. 'There's a nasty insect.' She flapped her arms wildly and ducked under her desk.

Nid reached the halfway point and paused for a moment behind a box of pens. The sharpener was heavy.

'It's a bee-eetle,' shouted the other girl. 'A big beetle with legs.'

Mr Binding stood up but he didn't move.

The girl under the desk screamed louder and Conor threw his exercise book at the window. It crashed against the pane, just missing Nid and knocking over the box of pens.

'Quiet, everyone!' said Mr Binding. 'We must remain CALM.'

The word 'calm' sounded like the screech of a cat that had shut its tail in the door.

'Is . . . is there anyone who can catch the . . . beetle?'

Edie knew in that moment that Mr Binding was scared of insects and his fear of them might save Nid if she acted fast. She stood up. 'It's all right, sir,' she said. 'I'm good with insects. I don't mind them. I'll catch it.'

She plunged forward, pushing her desk out of the way, and grabbed at Nid. She held him fast in one hand and opened the window with the other and then, with a dramatic flourish, she pretended to throw him outside. 'All done!' she said, holding up her empty hand. 'Beetle's gone.'

Everyone believed her. There was a smattering of applause from the rest of the class and one of the girls said, 'Eeeuww! How could you touch it?'

Edie slammed the window shut and hurried back to her seat, keeping her closed fist down by her side. She dragged her rucksack alongside her knees and tipped Nid into it. He was still clutching the sharpener to his chest.

'Give this to the boy,' he said.

She took it from him and carefully drew the zip closed.

'VERY good, Edie,' said Mr Binding, looking relieved. 'Very good indeed.'

'I'll just clear up the pencil sharpeners for you, sir,' Raphael said, already down on his hands and knees and slipping a sharpener into his pocket. It wasn't quite the mission that Nid had planned, but Raphael would still end up with a sharp pencil.

*

Today was a half-day because of a parents' meeting for Year Tens, so everyone was allowed to leave at lunchtime.

Edie ran out of school ahead of everyone and rushed round the corner to catch the first bus. As Nid had come into school with her they could go straight to Ada's charity shop. She clambered up onto the top deck and sat down right at the back.

'Nid? Are you there?' she whispered, easing the zip on her rucksack open again.

His face appeared at the gap. 'I was only trying to help.'

He was clutching the boiled sweet that was now the size of a Smartie. A bin lorry stopped to empty the school bins and the bus shuddered to a halt. Crowds of schoolchildren were gathering at the next bus stop and Edie's plans of a quick getaway were scuppered. There was a clatter of feet as some of them came up the stairs to the top deck. Naz appeared first with two other girls, followed by Linny and Conor, the boy in her maths class.

'Hi, Edie. Didn't realise you were so good with insects,' said Linny, all fake friendliness. They draped themselves over the seats around her.

She heard Conor whisper 'Flapper' to Linny. During the early weeks with the too-big shoes Edie had been called Flapper and the name had stuck. Linny laughed a tinkly false laugh.

Edie stuck her feet out into the aisle to show them that she had new shoes with laces and thick soles, but Linny pretended not to notice.

'Leave her alone,' said Naz suddenly.

Linny ignored her and blew a bubble of pink gum. It smelt of sickly sweet cherry.

'Guess what Edie did today?' she said.

'What?' said Naz, who was in a different maths set.

'She caught a beetle and threw it out of the window.'

'That's impressive!' said Naz.

'So now Edie is Mr Binding's pet,' Linny went on. It felt like the sting in her tale.

As usual Edie said nothing. Linny sucked the gum back into her mouth, chewing furiously until it was a tight ball. Then she pulled it out of her mouth and stuck it on the back of the bus seat. 'Edie loves Mr Binding!' she said in her annoying sing-song voice.

Edie felt the zip of her rucksack pocket being eased open and, glancing down, she saw Nid's head pop up between the teeth. He was watching Linny and scowling, and Edie couldn't help smiling at his loyalty.

'What's funny?' Linny asked, and Nid ducked out of sight.

'Nothing,' said Edie quickly.

Linny turned to the others. 'See. It's true. She *does* like Mr Binding!'

The ting of the bell went as the bus reached a parade of shops and the group gathered up their bags and began to move down the aisle. 'I'm going to get chips,' said Linny.

Nid wriggled through the gap in the zip and swung himself up onto the back of the bus seat in front of Edie. He stood beside the stub of pink gum and, pulling out a small toothpick from his bag, he angled it under the gum and flicked it upwards. The blob of gum shot down the bus and landed in Linny's long wavy hair.

The Year Sevens clattered back down the stairs. Naz was the last to go and for a moment she lingered on the stairs and looked back. Edie pulled Nid down out of view.

'See you, Edie,' she said, adding quickly, 'I like your new shoes.'

Edie was stunned. She lifted her arm and gave a small wave. For the first time she realised that maybe she was acting just like Linny and shutting Naz out.

Nid prodded her. He was perched on the sill of the bus window. Edie watched as Linny walked away from the bus stop and rubbed the back of her head. Edie imagined the gum slowly working its way towards the roots, making a deliciously sticky, tangly ball.

Chapter Twenty-Four

Baker Street

Found: four umbrellas, three raincoats, a trumpet, more gloves, a cat basket and a biscuit tin

A large sign was posted on the front of the charity-shop window.

Due to staff holiday the shop will be closed until 8 November.

Edie read it out to Nid. She had forgotten that of course Ada was away on her trip with Baby Sol's family and it would be a whole week before she was back. How could Edie find out where Juniper lived now?

She crossed the road back towards the Lost Property Office, fighting back tears of frustration. Yet again she checked @JunipBerry's Instagram account. There was one new comment that read: *Doesn't fool me, @JunipBerry. That pixie's made of plastic!* But Juniper seemed to have stopped posting.

The office was almost deserted as it was lunch hour. Dad was picking up sacks from London Bridge Station and she didn't want to risk going upstairs to look for Bead until she knew for certain that Vera was out too, so she joined Benedict at the sorting table in the basement. His bandage had been removed and he was lifting missing items off the helter-skelter.

'Cat basket . . . no cat. Brass trumpet in case. One glove – blue wool. One glove – red wool. Another glove – green leather. Hi, Edie – could you see if you can match this pile of gloves into pairs? I've got things to do upstairs.'

Edie nodded miserably and Benedict bounced off, leaving her alone. She lifted the brass trumpet out of its case and looked at her pale reflection in the shiny bell.

Nid hopped out of her pocket and up onto the sorting table. 'Don't be sad!' he said.

'But I was supposed to be protecting you. And now we might never see Impy and –'

'Don't say it!' said Nid. 'It's not your fault. Just . . . don't give up.'

He tried to make a game of matching the gloves, climbing inside a toddler's stripy one and setting it upright so it looked like a ghost hand walking about.

There was a clang from down the corridor as one of the doors to the storeroom shut, and Edie looked up to see Vera walking briskly towards them. Shadwell was perched on her shoulder and she was dressed to go out. This was surprising as she hadn't seen her come down by the lift or the stairs. At the sight of them Nid dropped the stripy glove and scuttled inside a green leather one.

'I didn't expect to see you here,' she said coldly. 'Shouldn't you be in school?'

'It's a half-day.'

'That's fortunate,' said Vera. 'I didn't like school.'

'Why?' said Edie.

'Mostly I disliked the other girls, and they disliked me.'

Shadwell hopped onto the table and began jabbing at the gloves and turning them over with his beak. In horror Edie realised that Nid's tiny foot was sticking out of the end of the green leather glove. She quietly placed her hand over it, relieved that Vera wasn't wearing her eyeglass.

'Why didn't you like the other girls?' Edie asked, sliding the glove off the table and into her pocket.

'They were frivolous and silly. I lived alone with my father and a housekeeper, and he didn't want me to make friends. I amused myself.'

'Oh!' said Edie. 'Did you –'

Vera cut her short. 'I must be off. An appointment. I'm away for the rest of the day. Come, Shadwell.' Vera leant forward so that Shadwell could hop up onto her arm, and Edie thought she caught a glimpse of the jewelled bird pendant around her neck.

'Oh, and before I forget. A new sack has just arrived upstairs,' Vera said. She turned to go. 'Shall I send it down the chute?'

Without waiting for an answer she click-clacked up the stairs in her regulation shoes and within seconds a sack came sliding down the helter-skelter.

Edie dragged the sack along towards the sorting table, noting that it was curiously soft and bumpy. She was about to call for Benedict when she felt something move under her hand. Her whole body fizzed. 'Nid!' she hissed at the green glove. Was it Impy and Speckle? Had they somehow found their way back? Impulsively she tugged at the string round its neck.

The sack burst open in her hands and a dozen magpins rose into the air, squawking and chattering loudly, flapping their green-feathered wings and waving their scaly claws in her face. She cried out and frantically swatted them away, but they fluttered round her head, nipping at her plaits.

They zoomed around the basement in a ball of feathers, pulling everything in their wake to the floor. A china candlestick smashed and a tin of buttons skittered around Edie's feet. Edie ran after them and watched helplessly as they flew through the storerooms like a fleet of small destroyer planes, pulling mobile phones, bunches of keys, bags, hats and coats off the racks, and sending everything cascading downwards.

'What's going on?' shouted Benedict coming downstairs, alerted by the sound of smashing china. He rushed back and forth trying to catch mobile phones and swatted at the air as the magpins flew around his head.

Edie followed the flock up the stairs to the main office and watched in a panic as they upturned almost everything, scattering tags and sacks, tossing teabags into the air and pulling the ordered ranks of lost property to the floor. They unpegged every lost shoe on the washing line, pulled the *We Return What You've Lost* poster off the wall and pecked at the photocopier button until the paper jammed and the copier made a loud beeping noise.

Then the birds flew on, gathering round the Cabinet of Valuables at the far end. In the mayhem Edie thought she saw Vera in her overcoat waving her arms by cabinet's glass door, but then she was lost in the swirl of birds. When Edie got there the door was wide open and the birds were grabbing at the booty. Vera was nowhere to be seen. The necklaces, rings and pendants glittered like tiny comets as they were carried up into the air by the birds.

'Stop!' shouted Edie, picking up a broom.

She charged at them, managing to herd them out of the door and onto the street. They flew full force along the pavement, ruffling papers and whipping people's hair up as they went past, and they disappeared into Baker Street Station like a band of urban pirates.

Chapter
Twenty-Five

Baker Street

Edie stood by the main door. She couldn't speak. The whole Lost Property Office was in chaos and the shelves of the Cabinet of Valuables were almost completely empty.

It was then that she remembered Nid. She hadn't seen him since the magpins burst out of the sack. She stood up and felt in her pocket for the green leather glove, but it wasn't there so she ran back down to the basement and scoured the floor, hoping it had fallen out. Gloves were scattered everywhere and the trumpet from before lay on its side.

'Nid!' she cried. 'Where are you?'

She ran to and fro, lifting chairs and raking through smashed china. She crawled under the sorting table where the gloves had been to see if the green glove was there. Once again she heard the tip-tapping of Vera's shoes, this time running down the stairs, so she withdrew further under the table and hid behind a crate. The footsteps paused at the bottom, presumably to check if anyone was around. Edie could see through the slats of the crate that Vera was still in her overcoat and hat, and she was also carrying a bag. She strode down the corridor between the two big storerooms and Edie heard the distinctive clang of the door to the Storeroom at the End and then silence. Edie waited for a few minutes and then crawled out from under the table and stood up. What if she had Nid in that bag? Or Shadwell was holding the glove in his awful jabbing beak? She followed Vera as silently as she could and listened at the door to the Storeroom at the End. She must be in there. Where else could she be? There was no other way out and Edie would confront her.

She unhitched the catch and pushed open the heavy iron door, but the storeroom was in darkness. She switched on the fluorescent lights. The items on the shelves sat still and mute. She called out to Nid, but there was no one there. The Storeroom at the End was completely empty. Vera had disappeared.

*

A strangled cry came from overhead. Dad had arrived back from London Bridge. Edie scurried up the stairs to find him staring at the Lost Property Office in disbelief as the door clattered shut behind him.

'What on earth has happened?'

'I-I don't know,' she stammered. 'They were in a sack and I let them out.'

'WHO was in a sack?'

'I-it was birds, Dad. I told you before . . .'

Benedict appeared from the basement storerooms, flushed with excitement and carrying a huge fly swatter.

'It was like a force field going through the office, Mr Winter. A real invasion. Everything flying everywhere. Maybe they're extraterrestrial?'

'Extraterrestrials? Don't be daft, Benedict,' said Dad. 'How on earth do we even begin to clear this mess up?' He looked dismally at the umbrellas scattered on the floor like spillikins and pointed a shaky finger at the Cabinet of Valuables with its glass door swinging open.

Even Benedict's naturally happy demeanour sagged into silent shock as they all stared at the empty cabinet.

'How did they break the lock?' said Benedict.

The front door opened again and a small tribe of adults walked in, carrying clipboards and dressed in official luminous Transport for London jackets. At the front of the formation was Ursula Slate. 'Just here for a quick tour with some transport officials,' she said and then stopped. There was a long silence as they too looked about them.

'Timing's not the best,' said Dad, trying to shield the now empty Cabinet of Valuables from her view.

'Yes, I can see that. It looks as if you've had a party up here, so we'll go straight down to the storerooms. Come along, please.' Ursula led the way downstairs to the basement with her arm raised in the air like a flag. Benedict made frantic gestures to Dad with his hands, silently mouthing '*No*', but it was too late – they could hear the official party reach the bottom and set off along the corridor.

There was an eerie silence. Benedict, Edie and Mr Winter stood in the main office frozen to the spot. It wasn't long before footsteps clattered back up the stairs and Ursula reappeared with the group. She showed the tribe of officials out of the front door and turned to Dad. 'I'd like a word, please, in my office – *now*.' Ursula's office was across the road so Dad followed her out.

Benedict turned to Edie. 'I can't believe what just happened. How did those birds get in?'

'It was *my* fault,' said Edie. 'They were in a sack and I let them out. I-I thought they were something else.' She felt confused. 'I-I've lost a green leather glove, Benedict. I have to find it. It's really important.'

'It'll be all right, Edie. Don't look so worried. I'll help you.' He took hold of the now-familiar, industrial-sized broom. 'Guess what my horoscope said this morning?'

'What?' Edie said weakly.

'*Whatever you do, don't flap!*'

Chapter
Twenty-Six

Baker Street

E die hunted desperately for the green glove. She looked through chaotic piles of raincoats and around the Cabinet of Valuables. All that remained there was a small silver spoon that she picked up and held onto as she made her way up to the first floor, to the smaller office with the kitchen and up again to Vera's tiny eyrie.

She caught sight of the magpin as soon as she reached the top of the narrow staircase. It was perched on the handle of the fire exit and a tiny figure dangled from its beak.

Was it Nid? Edie couldn't quite see as the bird beat its wings against the pane of glass in a bid to escape. Edie stood still and kept her eyes on the small figure. She wondered if it was the same bird that had come in through the window during half-term.

The magpin stopped flapping and stared back at her defiantly.

Edie pulled the silver spoon out of her pocket and held it out at arm's length. 'Drop what you've got and you can have the spoon.'

The magpin hopped along the bar, still clutching its booty, but it cocked its head and looked at the spoon. The little figure didn't move. Edie twisted the spoon from side to side so that it glinted in the light from the overhead bulb. It was a beautiful spoon that had been engraved with leaves and polished until it shone. The magpin fluttered its wings again, reluctant to give up what it had, but it studied the spoon greedily as Edie pushed it closer towards it. Tempted by the shine, it darted in and snatched at it and the figure fell from its beak with a strange jangling sound.

Edie jumped forward and pushed down on the bar of the fire-exit door and the magpin turned and shot out through the gap in the door and down the fire-escape stairs. Edie dropped to the floor and picked up the small figure. It was stiff and cold and it wasn't Nid at all, but a toy action figure attached to a key ring.

Edie ran out onto the fire escape to see where the magpin had gone. It hadn't flown upwards into the sky, but was down at the bottom of the stairs in the yard playing with the glittery silver spoon. Edie called out to it in frustration. 'What have you done with Nid?'

The magpin looked at her quizzically, then snatched up the spoon and slipped through the grating of a drain, which seemed odd behaviour for a bird. Then she remembered Bead and, pulling the fire door shut behind her, she hurried into Vera's office and opened the desk drawer. There was nothing in it, not even a box of sugar lumps. Bead had disappeared and with him all chance of finding out what might have happened to Nid.

'Edie!' Benedict was on his way up the narrow stairs. 'What are you doing up here?' She swung round as he appeared in the doorway, trying to think of a reason to be there, wanting so much to tell Benedict that Vera had magically vanished from the storerooms and to ask him if birds ever flew down drains.

Before she could say anything, Benedict held up a green leather glove.

'Is this what you were looking for? I found it behind the photocopier.'

'Yes! Yes, it is.' Edie took it from him and gently closed her hand over its leathery fingers. She turned away from Benedict so that he couldn't see her peeping inside. Nid was deep in the pocket of the thumb hole. He gave a small wave.

Benedict spoke again. 'Edie, I don't know why you're up here poking around in Vera's desk, but you should come downstairs. Your dad's back and it's not good news.'

Chapter Twenty-Seven

Baker Street

'As from tomorrow, Ursula's suspended me,' Dad said. 'And the office is closed for the rest of the day.'

'We'll clear the mess up, Dad, I promise,' Edie said.

'Is she FURIOUS about all the valuables?' asked Benedict.

Edie decided that he was enjoying the drama a little too much.

'Yes,' said Dad.

Edie felt a horrible chill. This was getting worse by the minute. She went over and covered Dad's hand with her own. 'I'm sorry, Dad,' she said. 'This is all my fault. We'll sort everything out and prove to Ursula that you can be manager again.'

'Quick as a flash of lightning!' Benedict added.

Dad smiled weakly, but Edie could see that he didn't believe her. He looked pale.

Benedict patted him on the arm and pointed to the slogan on his T-shirt. *Don't Let the Muggles Get You Down.*

Edie stood up. 'Dad, I think you should have a rest for the remainder of the afternoon. We'll clear up.'

'I do feel a little faint,' said Dad, allowing himself to be helped through to a small staffroom at the back of the office. He lay down on the sofa and sipped a mug of sweet tea. Within minutes he had fallen asleep.

*

For the next few hours Edie and Benedict swept and mopped and cleaned and re-sorted every single item, putting them all back on the shelves. They made sure every shard of glass was picked up, they unjammed the photocopier and stuck the *We Find What You've Lost* poster back on the wall. Once Nid was reassured that the magpins had gone, he climbed out of the glove and collected all the spilled buttons and paper clips. He also found a single green feather by the rack of umbrellas that he gave to Edie. She could see straight away that it matched the one on Vera's hat.

It was late afternoon when they finished and almost dark. Edie carefully put Nid back inside her coat pocket where he promptly fell asleep. She was alone in the main office, wiping up the last of the spilt milk as Benedict had gone to put the brooms away and check up on Dad, when the bell rang on the front desk.

A boy was standing there in a hoodie that was a bit small for him and trousers with a lot of pockets. His arms seemed too long and poked out of the sleeves and he had curly dark reddish-brown hair.

'Have you come to report something missing?' Edie said. She picked up a pencil and a new form to take down his details just as she had seen Benedict do.

'Yes,' said the boy. 'I think it was left on the Underground.'

'What was it?'

'A box. A large wooden box with a lock.'

Edie felt her heart bumping against her ribs. She looked up and stared at him. Could this boy be Charlie?

'What was inside?' she said slowly, pretending to scribble down some notes on the report form.

'I-I can't really say what there was exactly,' the boy said.

At that moment Dad appeared in the doorway, looking a little more like his usual self. He was pulling some keys out of his pocket. 'We're closed, I'm afraid,' he said to the boy.

'He's reporting something missing,' said Edie, but Dad was firm.

'I've had quite enough today, Edie. Someone else on the team will have to deal with it. You and I won't be here for a while.'

'But, Dad!'

'No buts, Edie. Sorry, young man. You're too late. You'll have to come back another time.' He opened the door and ushered the boy out.

'Did you say your name was Charlie?' Edie called after him.

The boy turned back and looked at her strangely. 'I didn't say anything about my name, but yes my name *is* Charlie. Charlie Spring.'

Chapter Twenty-Eight

Alexandra Park Road

Dad sat like a crumpled dishcloth at the breakfast table. His shoulders sagged as he scraped his burnt toast. Edie had got up first thing to mop the kitchen floor and lay out breakfast and to walk Bilbo round the block. Her maths homework was laid out on the table. She was trying to make amends.

'I'll be late back from school today, Dad,' she said.

'Edie, you are forbidden from going to the Lost Property Office for the rest of the week.'

'I know, Dad, but it's trampoline club today.'

It wasn't altogether a fib, as trampolining club was on Tuesdays and Thursdays, but she wasn't actually going. She couldn't let another day go by with Jot and Flum missing and Impy and Speckle stuck with Juniper. She had to prove to Nid that she wasn't giving up on them and the one thing she could do was ask Charlie Spring for his help. She knew now that he cared as much about the flits as she did, because he had come all the way to the Lost Property Office to find them.

'All right,' said Dad. 'But be home by six.'

He fondled Bilbo's ears and looked out of the window. Edie knew he was wondering what he was going to do all day.

*

The school day was dragging on and on. At break time Edie sat on her usual bench over by the science block and watched a knot of Year Nines play basketball. Nid was in the front of her bag but had kept his promise to stay hidden.

In the distance she could see Linny and one of the other Year Seven girls. Linny was pretending to walk up and down as if she were on a fashion catwalk. She swung her ponytail from side to side. Edie noticed that it looked shorter than before and wondered if the chewing gum had anything to do with it.

The bench creaked slightly as someone sat down beside her. It was Naz, and she was slightly out of breath.

'Hi, Edie. Do you always sit here?'

Edie immediately felt defensive. 'Not always,' she said.

'Did you like the chocolate spider?'

'It was OK,' Edie said, and half smiled.

There was an awkward pause. Edie remembered how she had felt on the bus and was about to say something else when she noticed Linny and the other girl walking across the playground towards them. Linny began to exaggerate her footsteps and sashay her hips.

'Did you tell them I was here?' Edie said. She felt cross and prickly as once again she doubted Naz.

'No. I promise I didn't, Edie. I left my jumper in the science block and I saw you through the window. I'd been wondering where you go during break.'

Now both Linny and her friend were doing the fashion catwalk and then they waved their feet at Edie as if they were making fun of her shoes again.

'What do you want?' Edie said.

'I just wanted to say –' Naz waved her hand towards Linny – 'that she's not as great as she thinks she is.' There was a pause and then she continued. 'Please can we do something together? Maybe on Saturday morning?'

Edie looked at Naz. 'With Linny?'

'Nah,' said Naz. 'She's going to the high street with some of the girls. It's a bit boring. We could go to the pool. You know, like we used to?'

For a moment Edie wanted to say yes. She longed to go swimming with Naz and forget all about Juniper, to do backflips off the edge and make faces at each other underwater, but then she thought of how the term had begun. Naz had been part of all that.

She felt uncomfortable and confused, but her *real* friends were in trouble. 'I can't,' she said. 'I'm doing something else.'

For a moment Naz looked hurt but then she shrugged her shoulders. 'All right. Another time maybe?'

Edie said nothing. It was easier that way.

'See you.'

As Naz left Edie looked down at her phone. @JunipBerry's Instagram account was active again. She lifted Nid out of her bag and together they looked at the posts. Speckle was wearing the pixie suit and sitting on a toadstool and Impy looked furious in a strange tutu dress. The caption read: *Be ready, believers. Not long until my big fairy show.*

'What does that mean?' asked Nid.

'The *big fairy show*.' Edie felt panic grip her chest. What *did* it mean? Maybe Impy and Speckle were going to be sold to a collector? Only two more lessons to go and they could go to High Barnet again. Edie felt sure that if she could find Charlie Spring he would help them.

Chapter
Twenty-Nine

High Barnet

It was dusk by the time they reached High Barnet and the lights were on all over Charlie's house. She rang the doorbell and Ivan answered. He took one look at Edie and her school uniform.

'You again. You want Charlie, I suppose,' he said in a bored voice and called up the stairs.

The boy who had come to the Lost Property Office jumped down the last three steps and came to the door. He had taken off his school jacket and shoes and Edie could see his odd socks. He looked at her strangely as if he knew he had met her somewhere before but couldn't place her.

'My name's Edie Winter,' Edie blurted out. 'My dad works at the Lost Property Office and it was me who you spoke to last night. My dad told you to come back?'

He nodded quickly. 'Yes . . . I remember,' he said. 'I went early this morning before school, but they said the box they had listed had gone missing. Have you found it?'

'Sort of . . .' said Edie. She was beginning to shiver in the damp night air. 'Is there somewhere we could go . . . to talk?'

Charlie looked over his shoulder. His mum was in the kitchen and Ivan was draped over a sofa in the sitting room watching TV.

'What about your shed?' Edie said.

'How do you know about that?'

'Because I know that's where you kept the flits,' Edie said quietly.

Charlie looked startled and stared at her. Then, for the first time, he grinned. 'Come on then.'

Picking up his shoes and a torch, he led her down the side gate to the garden shed. The shed was quite large. It smelt of pine and was dry and warm, if a bit cobwebby. Rows of flowerpots filled two shelves. Edie jumped at a huge bird with frozen staring eyes and pointed ears that was looking at her from the back of the shed. Charlie shone the torch at it. Its body was like a windsock with feathers painted on it, and its wings lifted slightly in a draught from the window.

'That's Mum's Prowler Owl. It's not real. It scares the pigeons in the garden. Look.' Charlie picked up the Prowler Owl by its pole handle and, pumping it up and down, he made the wings flap convincingly. It was so real that Edie drew back, banging her elbow on a pile of flowerpots. Charlie put it down and pulled out two old garden chairs. He sat in one of them, looking up at her expectantly.

Edie sat down and unzipped the front pocket of her bag. 'Nid? You can come out.'

Nid scrambled out of the pocket and cartwheeled across Edie's lap. He leapt onto Charlie's knee and did a star jump.

Charlie gasped. 'You found them!'

'Well, not quite,' said Edie, but Charlie wasn't listening.

He was holding out his hand for Nid to jump onto. 'When I got home and heard that Mum had cleared out the shed and given the box to Ivan I thought I would never see them again,' he said. 'Where are the others?'

'That's just it,' said Edie, trying to keep her voice steady. 'I-I've lost them.'

Edie told Charlie everything from the moment she saw the box on the Tube train with Impy inside it to Juniper and the fairy show, and Vera Creech, the spy bird and the strange invasion of magpins at the Lost

Property Office. The story tumbled out of her and she felt almost light-headed with the relief of being able to tell someone else.

'I've ruined everything,' said Edie. She showed Charlie the Instagram picture of Speckle and Impy with Juniper's latest caption about the fairy show.

'No, you haven't,' said Charlie matter-of-factly. 'We'll get them back. Let's send Juniper a message asking where the "fairy show" is.'

'I can't,' said Edie. 'She'd guess it was me. I don't want her to know that I'm even looking at these pictures.'

'Yeah, but she doesn't know who *I* am,' said Charlie. He pulled his own phone out of his pocket and posted a message.

I'm a believer, @JunipBerry. Where's the show? @CSpring

Charlie placed his phone face up on the shelf, and for a few minutes there was nothing. Charlie picked up his skateboard and pushed Nid around on it and Edie tried to avoid looking at the Prowler Owl in case it had moved. The phone lit up and gave a light ping. Juniper had posted a slightly fuzzy image of an advert.

Winter Fair
Frederick Hall, Crystal Palace
Saturday 6 and Sunday 7 November 10 a.m.
Come and marvel
Small Worlds and Magical Places
Bring all the family

At the bottom Juniper had posted the caption: *My mum's friend runs it and she's given me MY OWN 'fairy show'. See you there @CSpring.*

'So *that's* what she means by the "fairy show",' said Edie. 'And it's this weekend.'

'And that's how we'll get them back,' said Charlie.

Chapter Thirty

High Barnet

It was Nid who reminded them there was something else they could do now.

'We could see if Jot's left a message?'

They ran together down the pathway with Nid clinging to the seam of Charlie's pocket. It was nearly dark and the station was almost deserted. Edie checked her watch. Four forty-five. She would easily be home by six. One train sat at the platform with its doors open, waiting to go, as Edie showed Charlie Jot's name. The sugar was still there, uneaten.

The train driver stuck his head out of the cab. 'You comin'?' he shouted.

'No thanks,' said Charlie.

The train doors clattered shut and it pulled out of the station. Rain started to fall in big sloshy drops.

'I'll keep checking,' Charlie said. 'I can come every day.'

Nid clambered down onto the bench, and pointed to some faint scratchy writing just above it. It looked as if it was written by the stub of a pencil. Charlie flicked on his torch and they crowded round the wall.

Jot is a prisoner. Magpins got him. He is at Wilde Street Station.

They scoured the wall, looking for other messages or some other sign. Who had written this?

'Where's Wilde Street?' said Charlie.

There was an Underground map further up the platform and Charlie and Nid began tracing the different coloured lines to find Wilde Street Station. Edie thought she knew the names of almost every station, but this one confused her.

She noticed a forgotten umbrella lying on the bench and picked it up, thinking how it might please Dad if she found something for the Lost Property Office. The rain was now heavy and sliding down the back of her neck, so she slid the umbrella out of its cover and tried to open it. It jammed slightly so she ran her hands down the spokes, and her fingers caught on something. Curled round a spoke and fast asleep was another flit.

'Charlie! Nid!' she called out.

The umbrella swung in front of her like an empty

teacup. A drop of rain fell on the flit and it woke up. It was a girl flit not much older than Impy. Her hair was sculpted into spikes and there was a smear of dirt across her cheek. When Charlie loomed into view the flit pulled out a needle from her backpack and pointed it at them.

'It's OK!' said Edie. 'We're not going to hurt you. We were looking for Jot.'

'Jot?' said the flit. The needle wavered slightly.

'Yes,' said Edie. 'Was it you who wrote on the wall?'

'Might have been,' said the flit. On her chest Edie could see an F7 badge.

'What's your name?'

'What's yours?'

'It's Edie.'

The flit said nothing, so Nid slid into the bowl of the umbrella and stood up beside her.

'This is Jot's brother,' said Edie.

The rain was getting heavy and drenching the flits.

'Shall we go somewhere dry?' suggested Charlie.

The flit gave a tiny nod, so Edie carefully folded up the umbrella with the new flit and Nid inside and they returned to Charlie's shed.

*

'I'm hungry,' the new flit said as she settled cross-legged on a flower pot. 'Got any fried chicken scraps?'

'Didn't you eat the sugar we left for Jot?' Nid said.

'Nope. Don't like sugar.'

Nid looked at her, amazed.

Charlie dug in his pockets, pulling out string, a head torch, a spanner and a packet of mini cheese biscuits. He offered one to the new flit and she stuffed one in her mouth, filling her cheeks like hamster pouches.

'Can you tell us your name now?' asked Edie.

'It's Elfin,' she said between mouthfuls. 'I live in the vaults at Waterloo Station.'

She took another biscuit from the packet. 'Jot told me about you,' she said, pointing at Nid. 'He said he had a sister too and a twin brother.'

'Where did you meet him?' Edie asked before Elfin could say anything else.

'He was lost. He'd taken a wrong turning at King's Cross and found himself at Waterloo. He was hungry so he came back and had some food with us, but he wanted to get back to Hillside to see if he could find your flum. I showed him the way. Couple of days later I got the message via the Underground mice that he'd got himself caught by one of the magpins and taken to the ghost station at Wilde Street. And he wanted me to come all the way to High Barnet to let you know.'

'Of course. Wilde Street! It's a ghost station,' said Edie. 'That's why it's not on the map.'

'Yeah, that's right. All the scavengers and thieves end

173

up in those old empty stations. No one ever goes there and most of them are bricked up. The magpins chose Wilde Street. Trying to undo the hard work we do recycling and cleaning up the litter – and stealing our baby flit nuts.'

'Why do they want them?' asked Nid.

'Someone wants to use them as pickpockets when they've hatched. Tiny fingers. Invisible to adults. What's not to like? Easy pickings, isn't it?'

'What should we do?' said Edie.

'We're going to attack. Saturday night. Try to rescue Jot and all the other missing young flits.'

'We'll come too,' said Charlie.

'Have you got weapons?' asked Elfin.

'Yes,' said Charlie firmly.

Edie felt light-headed with a renewed sense of hope.

'Right, come to Waterloo railway arches on Saturday afternoon. Far end of Leake Street.' Elfin stood up. 'I have to get back now.'

'How will you go?' asked Edie. 'It's a long way to fly.'

'I ride on top of the trains,' said Elfin. 'Hook myself on with this.' She pulled a ring pull from a can out of her bag.

'You ride *on top*?' breathed Nid.

'Course. It's easy when you know how. Can be a bit windy, though. High Barnet to Waterloo. Takes you less than an hour. Never *inside* the trains, though! Too easy to get splatted against a window. I was just hiding in that umbrella until the rain stopped.'

Nid looked at Elfin with shining eyes as she stood up and flitted off through the hedge on the way to the station. 'Wo-ow!'

'Come on,' said Edie. 'We've got to go too.'

Chapter
Thirty-One

Alexandra Park Road

They made it back to Edie's street just before six, but Edie felt uneasy. She had no idea how she was going to persuade Dad to let her go to the fairy show in Crystal Palace at the weekend and to Leake Street to see Elfin. Not after everything that had happened. She didn't think she could bear the disappointment.

Dad opened the door, looking completely different from the man she had left that morning. Ursula seemed to have been forgotten and his suitcase was standing in the hallway. It turned out there had been an urgent call from Mum.

'I'm going to Finland first thing tomorrow,' he said. 'Granny Agata fell again this morning and has broken her leg. Mum and I are going to bring her here to recuperate.'

Edie tried to think about Granny Agata, but a hundred more thoughts raced through her head. How could she possibly look for Impy if Dad planned on taking her to Finland *too*?

'What about me?' she said.

Dad looked at her blankly.

'I can't miss school.'

If it wasn't for the flits, a week off school would have been the best thing ever.

'No, of course not!' Dad said. 'You're not coming, Edie. Benedict's going to stay for a few days. It's all arranged.'

Edie felt sorry about Granny Agata, but she also couldn't believe her luck.

*

Dad left for the airport very early the next morning and Benedict was installed in the kitchen by the time Edie arrived home from school. He had brought with him a rucksack full of clean T-shirts, a packet of sparklers, a guide to British birds and a surprising array of cooking implements. His T-shirt for the day read *Yes, Chef!* and for their first evening meal he prepared a risotto, chopping and slicing peppers and onions into tiny neat squares, and gradually stirring the rice into a creamy dish. Nid watched from the sugar bowl.

'We've got a new manager and she's awful. Even worse than Ursula,' Benedict said. 'And everything's a gigantic muddle after those birds came in.' He took a breath. 'Look at this, Edie.'

He took a copy of the *London Herald* out of his bag and smoothed out the front page. Edie caught the words 'bird attack'.

Londoners continue to complain of birds flying through the Underground tunnels and causing disturbances. These birds are small with orange beaks and are scavengers, but experts have been struggling to say what type of bird they are, and whether they have anything to do with the extraordinary rise in thefts and pickpocketing recently.

Benedict patted his guide to British birds. 'I've looked at them all. Blue tits and goldcrests, greenfinches and chaffinches. None of them fit the description at all.'

'They're magpins!' Edie blurted out and Nid jumped up and ran behind a jam jar. 'They have something to do with all the stuff that's going missing. And so does Vera!'

'W-wait a minute,' Benedict said. 'Vera's a bit odd, but I doubt she's involved in all this. And what are *magpins*?' He picked up his book and looked under M.

'Magpie, mallard, moorhen . . . Are you sure you don't mean "magpie"? They're quite large and black and white.'

'No,' said Edie. 'I don't think you'll find them in any

books.' She longed for Benedict to be twelve rather than nineteen so that she could tell him about the flits.

*

It was getting dark and they could hear the Bonfire Night fireworks beginning to pop and bang in the display up at Alexandra Palace. Benedict flung on his coat and picked up the packet of sparklers. 'Let's go up to the top of the road to watch them.'

They stood at the end of the street and Edie lifted Nid onto her shoulder so that he could see the shower of lights exploding above them. Benedict handed Edie a sparkler and they each wrote their names in the air in zigzagging lines of white sparks. Edie wrote the name I-M-P-Y in big letters, looping and stretching her arm upwards and outwards to show how much she cared.

Chapter Thirty-Two

Alexandra Palace to **Crystal Palace**

'I thought I might come along too,' said Benedict. 'Just for the morning. I've got to see my mum this afternoon and she lives in South London.'

He was standing in the kitchen mixing pancake batter early on Saturday. Charlie and Edie stared at him. Edie had told him that they were going to a fun fair at Crystal Palace and Charlie had arrived first thing as they had planned.

As Benedict flipped a pancake he said, 'What you might not know about me is that I love roller coasters! It's a bit of a hobby. So I'll drive you there and go for a ride. How's that for a bargain?' It was difficult not to agree, especially after Benedict disappeared upstairs and

returned wearing a T-shirt that said in big letters across the front: *Today Will Be a Roller Coaster Ride!*

Charlie crumpled into laughter, but Edie felt tense. Today was their one chance to get Impy and the flits back and she couldn't let Benedict spoil it.

*

Benedict parked his yellow Mini near the top of Crystal Palace Park and stood looking out over the fairground. All the rides were spread out beneath them, humming and whirring in a sea of flickering neon lights and tinny music. The smell of burnt sugar and popcorn drifted up the hill towards them. Edie could see the big wheel

181

with its umbrella seats, dodgems with electric points that crackled and sparked and, towering over them all, a roller coaster with loops of red track.

Benedict was already heading downhill. 'Big wheel first,' he said.

They rode on the big wheel and banged and bashed their way around the dodgem track twice. Nid loved the fun fair. He climbed up the sparking pole at the back of the dodgems, urging them to go faster.

'Are you coming?' Benedict called over his shoulder as he set off towards the roller coaster. It was the most popular ride and a queue of people snaked its way round the fence. It was going to be a thirty-minute wait at least.

'Now's our chance,' whispered Edie.

For a moment Charlie wavered as the roller-coaster cars swooped above his head. Even Nid was tempted.

'Charlie!' hissed Edie.

'Nah!' he said. 'I'll stay with Edie.'

'OK,' said Benedict. 'I'll see you in an hour.'

They turned away from the roller coaster and walked quickly across the fairground towards the high street. They had worked out that Frederick Hall was somewhere at the far end of the street, but the pavements were crowded with families walking towards the funfair.

Edie gripped Charlie's arm. 'Look!' she said, pointing above people's heads.

A huge banner was hanging from the side of a large stone building about a hundred metres in front of them. *Winter Fair – Small Worlds and Magical Places* was written in bold brightly coloured letters. Fairy lights were strung round the door and people were queuing to go in.

'I just hope they're here!' whispered Edie as they waited to buy a ticket.

Tinsel and more fairy lights were draped across the doorways and round the walls of a large hall.

Running right round the edge was the first of the 'small worlds' – a train line with platforms and signals, railway workers, station buildings, clusters of cottages and fields with cows in. A steam train the size of a toothpaste tube rattled past, pulling six coaches behind it, whistling and belching steam as it went.

Stalls with small theatrical stages dotted the rest of the hall, displaying miniature street scenes, gardens and a banquet with tiny plates of roasted meats and cake. There was a racetrack with wind-up horses, a police station equipped with little whistles and helmets and a hairdresser's peopled by tiny rabbits. Right in the centre of the hall stood a huge doll's house with four floors of perfectly furnished rooms and gold taps in the bathroom. Knots of visitors crowded round every exhibit.

'This is brilliant!' said Charlie. He stared in at the bathroom, touching a golden tap with his little finger.

Edie was scanning the room for Juniper. Her eyes came to rest on a crowd of children in the far corner. She took a sharp intake of breath when she heard a familiar bossy voice. 'Come along, please. Be amazed at my real-live fairy show.'

'Charlie,' she hissed. 'I think Juniper is over there. Can you go and look?'

She felt Nid take a flying leap from her pocket over to Charlie. 'Don't let anyone see you, Nid,' she whispered. 'There are children everywhere.'

She watched as Charlie pushed his way through the crowd to stand at the edge of the semicircle. He stood on tiptoe for several minutes and when he came back he spoke quickly.

'I saw them,' he said. 'Both of them. She's put them in a weird sort of fairy display. And Juniper's all dressed up too. Nid's still there hiding under the podium.'

Edie was so desperate to see Impy again that she pushed her way through the adults and knelt down so that she was hidden behind a girl in a Puffa jacket. She peered between the heads of the smaller children.

A glass tank stood on a table covered with wire netting and, on the base of the tank, there was a scattering of rocks and pebbles and a fairy pool that had been lined with silver foil. Clumps of moss were stuck to the largest rock with glue, and the plastic toadstool from the Instagram picture was positioned on a dot of Blu Tack. Juniper had painted a small screen with watery splotches of green just behind it and stuck on some cut-out butterflies. Edie felt sick. It looked awful. A crude sign was pinned to the front of the glass tank.

Real-live fairy glade. 50p a look. Children only!

Juniper stood slightly to one side of the tank wearing a shiny green ballgown with puffed sleeves and clutching a plastic wand with a star at the top that lit up when she pressed a button. In her other hand she held a feather. She waved the wand wildly from side to side.

'Oh, little fairies, I summon you to the fairy glade,' she said in a tremulous voice. 'Come forth, Goatsbeard!'

'Goatsbeard?' Edie crinkled up her face in disgust.

Speckle suddenly appeared from behind the screen dressed in the red pixie hat and coat. He skipped round the fairy pool and made a few tentative star jumps. Next Juniper invited the audience to meet 'Blossom' and Impy appeared with an upturned buttercup on her head and a furious scowl on her face. She stomped her way across the tank and plonked herself down on a pebble. It was all Edie could do not to leap up and snatch the horrible wand out of Juniper's hand.

'Come on, little Blossom. Fly for the children,' said Juniper in her strange voice, and she tickled Impy on the nose with the feather. 'Look, isn't she pretty?'

Impy sneezed and turned her back on the audience. Juniper banged on the side of the tank and her voice became bossy and harsh as she prodded Impy with her wand. 'Fly, little Blossom.'

Slowly Impy stood up, pushing her buttercup hat out of her eyes. She fluttered her wings and lifted up into the air with her arms folded in front of her chest.

Edie had to bite her lip in order not to shout out. It was then that she saw Nid clambering up the slippery folds of Juniper's shiny ballgown.

One of the children cried out. 'Look . . . another fairy! On your dress!'

Juniper took this turn of events in her stride and, ever the impresario, she gleefully introduced a third act, snatching Nid up by the seat of his trousers.

'And here is Cowslip, who likes to try to escape. No you don't! Naughty Cowslip!'

Jamming a petal hat on Nid she lifted the netting and dropped him into the tank with the others, resealing the top. When the other two saw Nid they rushed over to him and Impy flung off her buttercup hat so that she could envelop Nid in her arms. Nid couldn't resist a circuit of cartwheels round the tank.

The children gasped, laughing and clapping. The adults either marvelled at their imagination, cooing and whooping along with them, or peered into the tank frustrated that there appeared to be nothing to see and that they were left out of the joke.

'Thank you. THANK you,' said Juniper. 'That'll be fifty pence, please!'

Juniper had turned the flits into performing animals.

Chapter Thirty-Three

Crystal Palace

Edie knew she had to be very careful. Causing a scene in front of all the kids and their parents would only make them think she was stealing Juniper's show. She slipped away unnoticed and hurried back to Charlie.

'Now she's got Nid in there too! We have to get them out of there,' she hissed.

'But how?' said Charlie. 'I hadn't expected it to be this busy.'

'We need to create some sort of distraction,' Edie said.

Charlie looked around. At the far end of the hall was a 'kitchen cafe' selling fairy cakes, finger sandwiches and pots of tea.

'We could smash crockery?'

'It would make a noise, but it wouldn't be enough,' said Edie.

On one side of the hall was an archway that led through to a much smaller anteroom lined with cupboards and shelves. It was deserted. Charlie tugged at Edie's arm.

'There might be something in those cupboards we could use,' he said. 'I'll go and look. Keep a watch for me.'

Edie moved to the side of the hall beside a display of mice dressed in tiny Santa suits. From here she could see directly into the side room and she watched as Charlie checked through the first three cupboards. In the distance she could hear Juniper's bossy voice inviting more visitors to the *real-live fairy glade*. Charlie closed the first three cupboards, but spent some time rummaging around on the bottom shelf of the fourth. Edie could see one of the organisers circling the room and coming this way.

'Charlie,' she whispered sharply.

In seconds he had shut the fourth cupboard and was back at her side holding something under his jacket. The organiser wandered past them.

'I think I've got something that will cause just the sort of distraction we need,' he said quietly. He opened his jacket to show Edie a small megaphone, a box of matches and a firework fountain. On the side of the fountain was written *Chimney of Fire* in silver letters.

'It was in the Scouts cupboard,' he said. 'They must meet here. It was probably meant for a fireworks display.'

'What are you going to do with it?' asked Edie.

Charlie was already scanning the room. 'Just go and stand by that fire alarm,' he said. 'And when I give you the signal hit it!'

Edie went over and stood by a small square of glass on the wall. Beside it dangled a silver hammer. Excitement prickled at the back of her neck, but she also felt fear. Fear that Charlie's plan would go wrong and they would end up at the police station and would never see the flits again.

Charlie moved along the wall until he was standing by the miniature railway track, and Edie could see him waiting for the train to slowly loop its way towards them from the other side of the room. As it came closer she saw Charlie light the firework fountain with a match.

A small blue light flickered on the touchpaper as the model train came towards them, clickety-click, clickety-click, until it was only centimetres from Charlie. It drew alongside him and he jammed the lit fountain into the engine cab.

It ignited, and with a fiery whoosh the train sped up and hurtled round the track, and a fountain of sparks shot up towards the ceiling. It spat and crackled and the Chimney of Fire became a huge column of gold and silver light. It was spectacular.

Charlie's plan had worked and he waved wildly at Edie.

I've always wanted to do this, thought Edie as she smashed the glass of the fire alarm with the hammer. Immediately the alarm sounded.

'Fire!' yelled Charlie through the megaphone. 'Please can everyone evacuate the hall? Evacuate the hall immediately.'

There was pandemonium.

The train was circuiting the hall with the Chimney of Fire reaching higher and higher towards the ceiling and smoke was beginning to billow about. There was a strong smell of gunpowder. Charlie grabbed Edie and pulled her behind the large curtain.

A fire warden in a high-vis jacket began herding stallholders and visitors towards the door. 'Right, everyone, outside, please. Neat and orderly!' she shouted above the constant ringing of the fire alarm. Crowds of people began to pour out.

In the chaos Edie looked round the edge of the curtain and could see Juniper arguing with the fire warden that she needed to take the glass tank with her, but it was too heavy to carry on her own. She lifted the lid of netting and tried to grab Impy and Nid, but they were too fast for her and scurried out of reach.

'I just need to find my mum's friend . . .'

'There's no time. Leave everything,' said the fire warden. 'Right now, please.'

'But there are fairies in there!' said Juniper, closing the lid again and wrapping her arms around the tank.

'Don't be so silly,' said the fire warden. 'At your age! Outside, please.'

Edie could see Juniper looking back towards the glass tank as she was herded outside. Slowly the hall emptied.

In the distance Edie could hear a siren.

'Get them,' hissed Charlie.

Edie slipped out from behind the curtain and ran to the tank, fumbling with the wire and tugging at it to release it.

Impy, Speckle and Nid were cowering under the plastic toadstool. As Edie finally managed to free the netting, Impy peeped out from under it.

'Impy!' said Edie. 'It's me.'

Impy's whole face lit up. She whooped and grabbed Speckle by the hand. Stretching out her wings she whirred out of the glass tank and, just for a moment, she hovered near Edie's face and touched her nose with the palm of her hand. 'I knew you'd find us,' she said.

'Quick, hide in here.' Edie opened her pocket and all three flits slipped inside.

As she spoke the Chimney of Fire finally spluttered out and died, though there was no one left to see it.

Charlie pulled Edie after him through the fire escape at the back of the hall and into an alleyway just as the wailing sirens made their way along the high street. 'Run!' he said.

They ran to the end of the alley and down a hill away from the high street, away from the crowds outside the front entrance and the gleaming red fire engines, and away from the confused firemen looking for the flames and finding only a fizzled-out firework rattling around in the cab of a model railway engine.

All Edie cared about was that she was running away from Juniper and that she had the flits warm and safe in her pocket. They ran down past the ranks of Victorian houses until they were back on the fringes of the park.

'Can we stop for a moment?' Edie gasped, sitting down on a bench. It was then she realised that Charlie was carrying the flit box.

'I found it under Juniper's table,' he said. 'But it's yours now, Edie. I'll tell the Lost Property Office.'

Edie opened her pocket a fraction and both of them peered in. Speckle scurried up onto Charlie's hand and Edie waited for Impy to appear, but she didn't come, so she opened her pocket wider and saw her crouched in a corner crying. Strong, clever, determined Impy was crying.

'*She made me dress up as a fairy,*' she sobbed.

'It's OK,' whispered Edie. 'You're safe now.'

Impy looked up with the same pair of eyes – fiercely bright – that Edie remembered from when she had first met her in the Storeroom at the End.

*

They returned with the flits to find Benedict (who had ridden on the roller coaster three times) and all headed back up towards the Thames in his buttercup-yellow Mini. His mum lived in Lambeth, so he agreed he would drop them at Waterloo for a couple of hours. The plan, Edie said, was to join the Saturday crowds on the South Bank of the River Thames and look at the market stalls and skateboarders. She didn't add that they were also going to the Vaults.

'As long as you stay with Charlie and don't do anything stupid,' Benedict said.

As Crystal Palace shrank into the distance, Edie itched to send Juniper an Instagram message, but she couldn't let Juniper suspect she had anything to do with the Chimney of Fire. Instead she wrote her message in the condensation that was misting up the windows of Benedict's Mini.

Her finger traced the letters: *So who is the fairy queen now?*

Chapter
Thirty-Four

Waterloo

The Vaults were a series of disused railway arches at the back of Waterloo Station. Pools of water stood in front of the arches and the bricks felt damp to the touch. Edie thought of the old marshlands of the River Thames deep under their feet.

They walked through Leake Street where graffiti artists had spray-painted the walls with giant neon lettering and technicolour signs. The flit box had remained in the boot of Benedict's Mini and Speckle had decided to stay inside it with his comforter walnut. Nid sat on Charlie's shoulder, staring at the graffiti.

'There it is!' he cried out when he spotted Elfin's name written in blue spray paint and he insisted on adding his own.

Almost as soon as he had finished, they heard a sharp whistle and Elfin appeared.

She took them through a narrow doorway that was hidden from the street and led into a small chamber. Edie could see an ancient-looking electricity generator and piles of junk – empty cans of paint, some old railway sleepers and panels of corrugated iron. The air smelt warm and a bit metallic, like pond water and spark plugs. Right at the back, against the brick wall, Elfin and the Vault flits had a camp.

Edie and Charlie knelt down. A match was struck on the side of a matchbox and held up like a fiery torch. It was difficult to see past the flame, but Edie could just make out figures ringed round them – a circle of what appeared to be about eight flits, all wilder-looking than Impy's family. Their clothes were camouflaged and muddied and, like Elfin, their hair was sculpted into spikes. A few of them had catapults stuck in their belts.

Nid looked at them in awe. Edie could tell he thought they were the most exciting flits he'd ever met.

A fire was lit and soup was warmed in a bottle top and handed out to them all, and Edie became aware of a row of sooty mice sitting in the shadows at the back. Their long tails were coiled neatly beside them.

Elfin drew a map in the earth by her feet, scratching out the names of Underground stations with a matchstick.

'This is where Jot and many of our missing young flits are being held hostage,' she said. She drew a cross on the line between Baker Street and Regent's Park.

'We now know from the mice that the magpins have their roost here at Wilde Street.' There was a squeaky murmur from the mice. 'It's an old station that's unused now, but it's also the secret

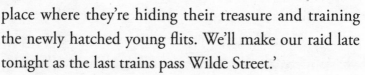

place where they're hiding their treasure and training the newly hatched young flits. We'll make our raid late tonight as the last trains pass Wilde Street.'

Elfin sketched out more of her plans on the dirt floor and turned to address the row of mice. 'How many can help us?'

'Easily a hundred,' said one of them. 'News spreads fast. We'll run along the tracks of the Bakerloo Line and be there.'

'What can you bring?' said Elfin, turning to Edie and Charlie and the Hillside Camp flits.

Edie reeled off a few items.

'Torches will be useful, but we need things to scare them,' said Elfin.

'I'll work on that,' said Charlie.

'Good. Are we ready?'

'Yes!' everyone assembled cried.

The Vault flits held up their needles and catapults and beat on some old tin cans with tiny sticks. Elfin handed Nid a catapult and told him to pick a cherry stone from a pile just beyond the fire. Nid was so excited he could barely keep still. He pulled the elastic back and fired a cherry stone hard at the brick wall. It pinged off the wall, ricocheting around the railway arch.

'How do we get to Wilde Street if the old station is closed up?' said Edie. 'We can't go through the tunnels.'

'I can ride on top of a train,' shouted Nid.

'No, Nid!' said Impy. The memory of the magpins chasing them on the night Flum disappeared still haunted her.

'Walk overground to Wilde Street,' Elfin said. 'You'll find the old station building. It'll be locked but you'll have to find a way down somehow. There's a maze of passage-ways down there. We'll meet you there at midnight.'

Chapter Thirty-Five

Alexandra Park Road

'Can Charlie stay over at ours tonight?' said Edie as the Mini rattled back over Waterloo Bridge. She tried to sound casual as if it wouldn't matter either way, but both she and Charlie knew that their adventure that night depended on it. Benedict hesitated, aware of his duties as a stand-in parent.

'I'll eat anything you put in front of me and do the washing-up,' said Charlie.

Benedict laughed and agreed, but only on the condition that they made a detour to Charlie's house so that he could meet his parents. As Benedict stood on the doorstep reassuring Charlie's mother that he was a reliable host, Charlie ran upstairs and reappeared several minutes later wearing his Scout trousers with pockets up the side and a rucksack that seemed to bulge in all directions.

'That's a lot of belongings for one night, Charlie,' said Benedict as Charlie squeezed back inside the Mini and waved goodbye to his mum.

Edie and Charlie glanced at each other and smiled. They had no idea how they were going to get into Wilde Street by midnight, but at least they were together.

Back home, Edie took Charlie upstairs to a bookshelf on the landing. It was known to the Winters as 'Dad's Train Shelf'. Dad loved everything to do with the Underground – the trains, the track gauges and the tunnels, and he had collected dozens of books. Edie read the titles aloud and Impy, Speckle and Nid ran along the shelves pointing out the ones that could be helpful, such as: *Adventures Beneath Our Streets* and *Haunted Underground*. At the far end, tucked in beside a 1950s map of the Tube, was a book called *London Underground's Abandoned Stations*. It was a large paperback book with photographs of the old abandoned stations, tunnels and lift shafts plastered across the front.

'Ghost stations,' said Edie. Immediately some of the names of the disused stations that Dad had once told her about came back to her. Down Street. Aldwych. British Museum.

'Dad told me lots of stories about ghost stations,' she went on. 'How they were used as air-raid shelters and secret government offices in the Second World War.'

The book had twenty-five chapters, each relating to a disused station. Many of the stations were bricked off and half demolished, and the old station buildings with their distinctive oxblood tiles had been turned into restaurants and shops.

Edie ran her finger down the list. 'Here it is.' She flicked to the page.

Wilde Street opened 1906. Closed 1939. Bakerloo Line.

There was a map showing the thin line of Wilde Street set in the tangle of streets just south of Baker Street and some black-and-white photographs of the station entrance and ticket hall as it had been in the early 1900s. Edie turned the page and there were more photos of the long curving platforms and stairwells and a figure in a bowler hat sitting on a bench. Speckle jumped onto the book and studied the photograph as if he might suddenly see Jot sliding down a stair rail or flying past a doorway.

Edie read on:

The station still exists at track level, although there is no access from the street. If you travel between Regent's Park and and Baker Street look out of the left side of the train, you can still see the platform and tiled walls.

Charlie pointed at a full-colour photo of the station as

it was today. The doors and windows were all boarded up. 'I don't think there's any way in,' he said.

'We have to find a way,' said Edie. She put down the book and started to pack her bag with things they might need. She put in two badminton raquets as swatters. 'What would magpins be scared of?' Edie asked him.

'Predators,' said Charlie. 'They'll probably be scared of cats, foxes and big birds of prey. Smaller birds don't like their eyes.'

Edie added a pocket torch and a head torch that had a switch to make the light blink. She wondered what was in Charlie's rucksack with its intriguing bulges.

Benedict called up the stairs. 'Your dad's on the line, Edie.'

It felt odd looking at Dad on the screen squeezed into Granny Agata's small kitchen in Finland. A jar of wooden spoons stood on the counter behind him.

'Hope you're not causing Benedict any problems,' he said as he eased Granny Agata's wheelchair into place. Her plastered leg stuck out in front of her and Edie noticed how thin she had become – all elbows and fingers.

She waved at Edie.

'Hello, Edie. Are you busy? Don't worry about school.'

Granny Agata had a habit of knowing when things weren't right without asking.

'I'm fine, Gran. School's OK. I'm making new friends.

I'm glad you're coming to stay for a while. Hope Dad's being helpful!'

'He is. The perfect house elf.'

Edie would have liked to ask more about Finnish house elves, but she knew that Charlie was waiting upstairs. 'I've got to go, Gran.'

*

'We should leave quite soon,' said Charlie.

They made up a sleeping-bag bed on the floor and stuffed pillows down it and under the duvet on Edie's bed to make it look as if they were both asleep. After a lot of swishing of the bathroom taps Edie called down the stairs.

'Good night, Benedict!' She could hear the television on downstairs as he was about to watch a spy film.

'Night, Edie!' Benedict called back. 'Teeth?'

'All done!'

Edie and Charlie got into their coats and lay on their beds in the dark, waiting. The flits put on hats and scarves and Nid armed himself with the catapult that Elfin had given him. At the last minute Edie threw her luminous cape into her bag.

At nine-thirty they crept down the stairs, past the sitting room where Benedict was watching television and into the kitchen. The film was in full swing with wheels squealing and horns blaring as a car chase unfolded on the screen.

Bilbo shifted in his basket and sat up, hoping that a squirrel expedition might be on offer. Charlie knelt and tickled his ears until he lay down again. He looked at them quizzically as Edie quietly unlocked the back door, letting in a sweep of cold night air.

Together they walked through the quiet streets past the garden centre to the Tube station at Bounds Green. A car went past, its tyres making a squashy sound on the damp tarmac. These were streets that Edie had known all her life, but the darkness and their expedition rucksacks made her feel as if she was walking into something completely unknown.

Chapter Thirty-Six

Alexandra Park Road to **Wilde Street**

At Oxford Circus they changed from the Victoria to the Bakerloo Line. The Tube trains were filled with crowds of Londoners out for an evening in town or returning from the Bonfire Night display along the River Thames. No one seemed to notice that two children were out alone.

As they headed north towards Baker Street from Regent's Park, Edie stood by the doors on the left-hand side of the train and stared out at the tunnel. The walls were caked in soot and dust and strung with long lines of power cables, but there was a sudden gap and she caught a glimpse of an open space in the gloom with shadowy shapes and the odd patch of green-and-white tiling.

'I think I saw it!' she whispered to the others.

It was dark and the train went so fast that it was difficult to know for certain. She had expected to see much more, imagining that the ghost station might reveal itself like a stage with magpins flying about and Jot trapped there waiting for them to free him.

At the top of the escalator at Baker Street Station Edie was the first to see Shadwell. He was hopping around near the entrance and distracted by a man selling hot chestnuts. Shadwell had one in his claw and was trying to peel off the hot shell with his beak.

Edie drew back and pulled at Charlie's arm. 'Quick,' she said. 'We have to go back down.' They withdrew into the crowd and rode back down the escalator.

'What are you doing?' said Charlie as they headed to the southbound platform.

'That was Vera Creech's spy bird and it mustn't, whatever happens, see us. It probably means she's somewhere nearby.'

Edie's nerves jangled like sleigh bells. A black umbrella dangling off someone's arm looked like a spy bird and a crumpled newspaper caught up in the draught from the tunnel resembled a magpin. As she looked back down the end of the platform a figure moved forward in a long coat and walked slowly towards them. Could it be Vera?

'We have to get out of here!' she said urgently.

They pushed their way to the front of the crowded platform and jumped onto the next train.

'But we're going back the way we came!' said Charlie.

'We can get out at Regent's Park and walk to Wilde Street from there,' Edie said.

The doors closed and the train picked up speed as it left the station. They found seats this time on the right-hand side and all pressed their faces to the window. Impy clung to Edie's collar and Speckle sat on the window ledge, but they were so busy looking out that they didn't notice Nid crawling up Charlie's jacket and standing on his shoulder.

'I can't see anything,' said Charlie.

'Wait,' said Edie. 'It's coming up. Any second now.'

Nid jumped up to the edge of the window, which was slightly ajar.

'Look, there it is now!' said Edie. The tiling flashed up again and this time she could just make out some steps.

'I'm going to ride on top of the train like Elfin!' shouted Nid.

He slipped through the window and launched himself into the darkness. Edie caught the flicker of his clothes as he catapulted downwards rather than upwards.

'NID!' Impy shouted and whirred upwards after him, but the rush of air at the window caught at her wings and pushed her back into the carriage. Charlie stared out at the walls of the tunnel, horrified, as the train rattled onwards. Impy tried to get out a second time and was buffeted back inside and Edie managed to snap the window shut.

'It's too dangerous,' Edie said, trying to keep her voice down as passengers in the train carriage were looking at them.

'Did you lose something out of the window?' a young woman asked.

'No. It's just an insect,' said Charlie firmly.

'Shall I squash it for you?' another passenger said, rolling up his newspaper.

'NO!' said Edie too loudly. 'It's fine. Thanks.'

Edie gently closed her fist round Impy to stop her battering against the window.

'Please, Impy. I don't want to lose you too.'

'But *I* can't lose Nid!' cried Impy from inside Edie's fist and she pummelled at the creases of her fingers.

A teenage girl stared at Edie suspiciously and whispered loudly to her friend, 'She's weird.'

As the train drew into Regent's Park, Edie stood up and moved to the doorway. 'We'll find him,' she whispered into her fist. 'We just have to get to Wilde Street as quickly as we can.'

Chapter Thirty-Seven

Wilde Street to **Baker Street**

A light rain was beginning to fall as they ran across the main road and into the streets around Marylebone. It was now quite late and people were spilling out of restaurants and bars.

'There it is!'

Charlie pointed up at the street sign – *Wilde Street W1* – and they turned into a quiet residential street. There was hardly anybody about.

The old station entrance was about halfway down, at the bottom of a mansion block. The deep-red tiles matched the photograph in Dad's book, as did the two half-moon windows with blackened glass that sat over the old entranceway. The words *Wilde Street* were still there, black writing on a white sign that was faded and chipped.

They ran over to the front of the building. All the windows at ground level were boarded up and at the left side there was a heavy wooden door that was locked and barred. Just to one side of it was a broken ventilation grille no bigger than a five-pound note.

'Any ideas?' said Charlie, wiping the grille with his sleeve and peering through it. 'We can't fit through this.'

Impy took off into the air. 'I can!' she called back, and without waiting for an answer she took a tiny, keyring-sized torch out of her bag and squeezed through the grille and disappeared.

'Impy!' Edie called after her. 'You can't go down there alone.'

Edie and Charlie pressed their faces to the broken grille and watched as Impy's light bobbed about in the dark. Speckle withdrew deep into Edie's pocket, unable to watch the last of his siblings vanish.

Charlie switched on his own torch and shone it inside. They could see the shadowy walls of an old ticket hall with its tiles and hatch. Impy's light fluttered onwards.

'Do you think Nid's OK?' Edie asked Charlie. Despite what she had said to Impy, she could still hear the screeching of the train's wheels as he tumbled out of sight.

'Yes,' said Charlie firmly. 'He'll have jumped out of the way doing a triple somersault or a crazy spinning cartwheel. I'm sure of it.'

He reangled his torch and the beam picked up a solid line of brickwork filling the far end of the ticket hall. 'Look, Edie. That's where the stairs would have been.'

As he spoke Impy's light bobbed its way back towards them and she slipped back through the grille.

'There's no way down,' she sobbed. 'It's all closed off. What do we do now?'

Edie patted Impy gently with the tip of a finger to try to soothe her. She had to think of something else fast. Deep beneath her feet a train rumbled through Wilde

Street like distant thunder and she thought of the tunnels and passageways zigzagging this way and that. There *must* be another way in.

Then she remembered the magpin.

*

'Down here!'

Edie had led them back up to the Lost Property Office past Baker Street Station. Impy had urged them all to run and Charlie was leaning against the wall to catch his breath. They were standing at the top of a narrow cobbled alleyway at the side of the building.

'What's down here?' Charlie gasped.

'I think there might be a passageway that will take us underground,' said Edie, keeping a careful watch for Shadwell.

She led the way through the alleyway and into the yard behind the Lost Property Office. The metal fire-escape staircase zigzagged up one side of the building and Edie glanced up at Vera's window. There was no sign of Shadwell on the sill, but the light was on. As they stood there it suddenly clicked off. She pulled Charlie back into the shadows, and they hid under the fire-escape stairs, waiting for several minutes.

'She might come down the stairs,' whispered Edie, but after a while, when nobody came, Edie gestured for Charlie to follow her and they crept over to the drain that the magpin had disappeared down. As they crouched down on the cobbles, they heard an echoey click-clack of footsteps. The sound was reverberating deep inside the drain. In fact, it wasn't a drain at all but a vent that led straight down into a tunnel.

A beam of light bobbed about the walls and a figure carrying a large bag passed beneath them, heading away from the Lost Property Office. Through the grating Edie saw the familiar streak of blue hair. Hopping along behind came Shadwell. He paused for a moment and shook out his wings.

Edie quickly drew back from the vent, sweeping Impy and Charlie back with her. She waited until the footsteps had died away and when she looked again Shadwell had gone.

'I knew it. There's a secret tunnel leading out of the Lost Property Office,' Edie said.

'But going where?'

'It could be to Wilde Street.'

'How do you know that?'

'I don't *know* for certain . . . but it would make sense.'

Charlie, for the first time, looked doubtful.

'Come on,' said Edie, pulling Charlie up the fire-escape stairs. 'We've got to go after her. It will lead us to the magpins and the missing flits. I'm sure of it.'

She pulled on the fire door, hoping it might still be

on the latch, but it was firmly closed. Pressing her face against the glass in the door she could see the bar handle inside. Charlie felt along the bottom where there was a gap and pulled a roll of string from one of his many trouser pockets.

'Where's Speckle?' he said and Edie lifted him out of her pocket.

'Can you take this end of the string and crawl under the door with it?'

Speckle nodded and gave a small salute.

'Then loop it over the bar handle inside and bring it back to me?'

Within seconds Speckle had done what Charlie had asked and reappeared under the door with the other end of the string.

'Come on, Edie,' said Charlie, and they took hold of both ends of the string and tugged hard. With a clank the handle inside was dragged downwards by the string and the fire door opened as if by a magical invocation.

'Brilliant!' said Edie and Speckle beamed.

The Lost Property Office was virtually in darkness, lit only by the dim glow from the safety lamps in the stairwells. They closed the fire door and walked over to the door to Vera's office. The light from her window cast a silvery glow across her desk as Edie quickly checked in her drawers for the eyeglass and Bead, but there was nothing there. As she turned to go, she noticed a birthday card propped upright.

Happy Birthday, Vera was scrawled across the inside, but it didn't say who it was from.

'No one mentioned it was her birthday,' said Edie. She thought back to Vera's comments about her strict father and lack of friends.

'Let's go-o,' urged Impy.

They went down the two flights of stairs to the main reception floor below. Edie switched on one of the side lights.

'Wow,' said Charlie, as he looked at the ranks of umbrellas and raincoats, and his hand rested on a forgotten Jedi fancy-dress robe that was folded on the desk ready for labelling. He was about to pick it up when he spotted the blue postal chute leading down to the sorting area in the basement.

'A helter-skelter!' he said, climbing up onto it.

'Charlie . . .!' hissed Edie, but she couldn't help laughing as he shot down the chute with Speckle on his shoulder. She knew it might be her only chance to try it too so she also scrambled onto the chute and shot down into the gloom after him with Impy, and they all ended up in a heap on the sorting table.

The outside door upstairs clattered and banged, and

Charlie and Edie slid off the table and ducked down underneath it.

'Was that the wind?' Charlie whispered.

A tentacle of fear wrapped itself round Edie's neck. Vera Creech and Shadwell were down in the secret tunnel surely? Maybe this was the magpins again or someone had seen them go up the fire escape and called the police. A key rattled in the lock and Edie heard the inner door swing open. Sweat prickled across her forehead.

They heard a voice muttering and the overhead strip lights burst into life. Footsteps came down the stairs.

'EDIE?' said a voice that was both urgent and angry.

Edie and Charlie crawled out from under the sorting table. It was Benedict.

Edie was speechless. Part of her was relieved it was Benedict and not anyone else, but how had he . . .?

'What are you *doing*?' Benedict said. He was wearing a bobble hat and the ribbon of keys to the Lost Property Office hung round his neck. Edie had never seen him looking so cross.

'How did you know we were here?' she asked.

'Bilbo started barking and fussing halfway through my film, so I went up to check on you both. Those pillows didn't fool me, Edie! Luckily I found that book out in the corridor – your dad's book about "abandoned stations" left open at Wilde Street. I went there and saw you in the distance running this way and then a light went on in here. What are you up to?' He stared at them both, wide-eyed.

They stood in silence with Edie's mouth opening and shutting like a fish.

'There's a secret tunnel,' said Edie finally. 'And we think it leads to Wilde Street ghost station and Vera –'

'What is it about Vera?' snapped Benedict. 'It's just all wild fantasy, Edie. What would your mum and dad think? And yours, Charlie! I'm supposed to be looking after you. We're going straight home now and you can explain everything when we get there!' Benedict turned to go, but Impy had flown over to him and was trying to lift the keys from round his neck. To Benedict they appeared to be lifting of their own free will.

'Uuuugh!' he said. 'What's going on?' He fell backwards, sprawling on the floor and clutching at his keys.

'Impy!' Edie whispered. 'Don't scare him!'

Charlie fetched a chair and a glass of water.

'It's not a wild story, Benedict. You have to believe us,' he said, helping Benedict up onto the chair.

'Vera was here earlier and she's been taking things from the Lost Property Office, I'm sure of it,' said Edie. 'She has some kind of control over the birds . . . the ones that are doing all the thieving. They live in Wilde Street ghost station.'

She told Benedict as much as she could without involving the flits – he was nineteen after all. Benedict sat very upright in the chair, clutching his keys in one hand and the glass of water in the other.

'You said yourself that the fire-escape door being on the latch the other day seemed odd.'

'Yes, but if you are so sure about all this, where is the secret tunnel?'

'I-I . . .' Edie had to admit she didn't know. 'It's here somewhere.'

'Right. Edie Winter, you have three minutes to show me the secret tunnel,' said Benedict. 'Otherwise I'm taking you home!' He began to count. 'One, two, three, four –'

'Come on,' said Edie, pulling Charlie and the flits after her. They ran into the first of the big storerooms, feeling along the walls and skirting boards for fake panels and checking behind the cupboards and shelves. In the second storeroom they moved huge baskets filled with hats and scarves to see if they had missed a secret doorway and Charlie knocked his hands along the plastering, testing if it was hollow.

'One minute forty-five, forty-six, forty-seven,' called Benedict in the distance.

'Are you sure it's here?' said Charlie as they paused to catch their breath.

'Yes,' said Edie, although now she wasn't sure at all.

They ran up and down the corridor, testing the floor to see if it was hollow and looking inside the broom cupboard where the cleaning things were kept.

'Two minutes!' cried Benedict.

'What's in here?' said Charlie, pointing towards the last of the storerooms.

'It's the Storeroom at the End,' said Edie, 'but I've already looked in there.'

'Let's try again.'

She opened the door and the light flickered on overhead. The rabbit alarm clock stared back at them mutely.

'Come on,' urged Edie just as Benedict cried, 'Two minutes and thirty seconds!'

They looked through all the shelves and Charlie climbed up to see if the air vent in the ceiling might open.

It was Impy who pointed to the Persian carpet on the floor. 'What's under there?'

Edie knelt down and started rolling up the threadbare carpet. As she did so the edge of a large trapdoor appeared.

Chapter Thirty-Eight

Baker Street to **Wilde Street**

'I can't believe it,' said Benedict. 'You'd never have known.'

They all stood in a circle looking down into the shaft of a tunnel. A series of metal rungs formed a ladder to the corridor below.

'We *have* to find Vera now,' said Edie. 'Please, Benedict. You have to let us go.'

'No!' said Benedict.

Edie turned away so Benedict and Charlie wouldn't see her cheeks flare red and her hot tears of disappointment. The silence was broken only by a distant siren.

Then Benedict spoke again. 'I meant, no, you are not going alone. I'm coming with you.'

Edie turned back and threw her arms round

Benedict's waist. It wasn't ideal having a 'grown-up' going with them, but Edie had always felt that Benedict was somewhere in between. 'Thanks,' she whispered, and she swept away her tears with the sleeve of her coat.

One by one they clambered down the ladder and into a long passageway. The air smelt stale like an old cupboard that hadn't been opened for years. Edie gave a head torch to Benedict and Charlie adjusted his and set off ahead of them, drawing a line along the wall with a piece of chalk so that they could find their way back.

They walked in silence and Edie felt water drip into her hair. Benedict brushed his face, leaving a sweep of sooty grime. The passage sloped downhill and the loud rumblings of Tube trains told them that they were getting closer to the tracks.

'Charlie,' Edie whispered. 'Come back and look at this.' She shone her torch onto the ground in front of her, picking out footsteps in the dust.

'But why would she come down here?' said Benedict.

They spoke in low voices so that the sound wouldn't bounce and echo off the walls.

'A ghost station is the perfect secret place as no one ever goes there. All those valuables that have gone missing from passengers – I think that's where they'll be hidden. And they're holding prisoners too.'

'Prisoners?' said Benedict. 'What sort of prisoners?'

Edie took a deep breath. 'They're called flits. Tiny people with wings. They live in a deserted station up at Highgate, but the magpins invaded their camp and some of them ended up in that box I found.'

'Edie, this is ridiculous. Vera is one thing, but tiny magic people?' said Benedict.

'You're too old to understand,' said Edie.

'Too *old*? My mum still calls me Peter Pan!'

'Stop, everyone,' said Charlie suddenly.

The tunnel had flattened out, but they had reached a junction and it split into three.

'Which way?' he said.

Edie looked at the footsteps in the dust. 'Take the one that goes straight ahead.'

After only a few metres, the rumble of trains sounded closer, as if they were running alongside them, and the beam of Edie's torch picked out a large red arrow on the wall. *Platforms This Way*. Just beyond it was an old Tube map.

'Must be getting on for a hundred years old,' said Benedict.

The Tube lines were disordered and tangled and very different to the map that Edie knew. She ran her finger along the rust-coloured Bakerloo Line with Impy perched on her knuckle. There it was – Wilde Street Station – one stop to the east of Baker Street.

A short flight of steps took them down to the trains. They walked through to the northbound side and stood on the deserted platform.

Impy called into the darkness. 'Nid? Nid, are you there?'

A familiar clicking of the tracks and push of warm air from the tunnel told them that a late-night train was coming. They drew back against the wall and switched off their torches.

The headlights of the Tube train swept into the station, and the lit windows of the carriages flickered over them like images on a film. In seconds the train was gone. The darkness was so dense that it almost felt thick enough to wear, and the stony smell reminded Edie of a graveyard.

Charlie flicked on his head torch again. 'This is wicked!' he said. He turned his head this way and that, picking out the old station signage and tattered 1920s posters and tiling in the beam. 'What time is it?'

'Ten to midnight,' said Edie.

'Ni-id?' cried Impy again.

'H-he's probably hiding somewhere,' said Edie. She didn't dare shine her torch down onto the train tracks.

'Who are you talking to?' asked Benedict finally. 'The tiny magic people?'

'Yes,' said Edie firmly, and Benedict merely nodded and didn't ask any more questions. She wondered for a brief moment if she could find him a *Peter Pan* T-shirt.

As their eyes grew accustomed to the gloom, they could just make out more passageways leading off from the platform, and right down at the far end something was glowing.

'Why is there a light?' whispered Benedict. 'Birds don't have lights. This is spooky.'

Chapter Thirty-Nine

Wilde Street platform

The light spilled out through an archway and just beyond it they could see an old signal box. Slowly, carefully, they crept along the wall and peered round the arch. It opened out into a large hallway where passengers must once have flooded down the stairs from the ticket hall above.

The interior was lit like a stage in a theatre. Two bike lamps dangled from hooks and in the shadows behind them there must have been fifty magpins perched on cables and ledges, roosting. The lamps were angled like miniature spotlights on a semicircle of old wooden tool crates, and the crates were filled to the brim with stolen goods. It was like a treasure haul that wreckers might have dragged up from the bottom of the River Thames.

'Whoa!' Benedict said.

Dozens of watches in gold and silver hung over the edges of one crate and rings with stones as big as boiled sweets lay scattered across the

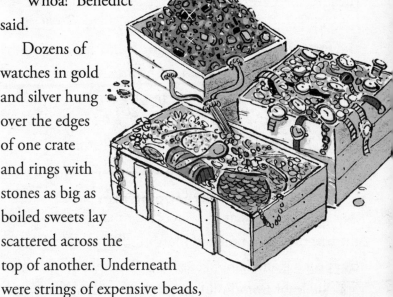

top of another. Underneath were strings of expensive beads, necklaces with pendants of blue sapphire and green jade, charm bracelets, handbags, watches and even a candlestick. In another crate embroidered purses, decorated boxes and spoons and even a spangled tiara sat piled up, glittering in the torch light. The magpins must have been thieving for weeks.

'This is crazeee!' Benedict whispered as they stood in the shadows, gawping. 'Just wait until they hear about this at the LPO.'

One of the magpins opened its eye and cocked its head, listening.

'Sssh!' Edie whispered, and indicated they should all move back down the platform. As she turned she dropped her torch. It clattered to the floor and the magpin flapped off its perch, giving an alarm call. Then the fifty or so other magpins lifted into the air and the station was suddenly filled with birds flying back and forth, screeching and calling to one another that there were intruders.

At that moment Elfin and the small troupe of Vault flits, armed with needles and catapults, emerged from the tunnel. They fired cherry stones and waved their needles like sabres at the screeching mapgins. In return the magpins dive-bombed the Vault flits and flew to and fro, pecking and flapping at Edie, Benedict and Charlie. Speckle leapt from Edie's pocket and took up a catapult and Impy made wild karate kicks, managing to catch a magpin under its beak and send it spinning.

Meanwhile, a sea of mice came swarming round the back of the signal box, dragging a long string of tin cans that clattered and banged around the station.

It was pandemonium.

'Now!' shouted Charlie. 'Let's bring out what we've got.'

Edie pulled a pack of super-sized sparklers out of her rucksack and gave one to Benedict.

'Use this to confuse them,' she said as she lit one of the sparklers, and she also handed him a badminton raquet. They walked out into the mayhem with Benedict's arms windmilling round him as he tried to swat away the magpins. Cherry stones pinged off their heads and smoke from the sparklers began to waft about.

'Owww!' said Benedict as a cherry stone hit him hard on the eyebrow.

His badminton racquet caught some of the birds and sent them tumbling. With the other hand Benedict swished the lit sparkler furiously this way and that as if he was a Jedi knight holding a glowing lightsabre.

'This is brilliant!' he shouted, but the birds hated the sparks and fizzing light.

Edie dragged her luminous cape out of her rucksack. She switched off the bike lamps and flapped the cape in the gloom so that it billowed out in a soft phosphorescent green like a ghostly flag.

'Get back!' she shouted angrily, thinking of the damage the magpins had caused to the Lost Property Office and Dad's reputation.

'Get back!' she shouted again, finding a strength in her voice that she never could at school. She flapped the cape at the dive-bombers, snapping the fabric like washing on a line in a gust of wind.

It was working. Several of the magpins began to retreat, circling into a tighter and tighter flock.

Out of the corner of her eye she could see Charlie bent over his rucksack. He pulled out the Prowler Owl from the garden shed and his skateboard. He held it up like a puppet over his hand, lighting the inside of its head with his torch. He started to lift the pole up and down so that its huge wings began to beat softly. The Prowler Owl's shadow ran up the walls of the chamber and slowly Charlie turned its yellow eyes on the magpins. Lit from within, they looked like headlights.

'Predator!' said Edie softly to herself.

Charlie stepped onto his skateboard and made the owl swoop to and fro as he skated backwards and forwards. Then he held a toy megaphone up to his mouth and breathed into it a deep ghostly hoot.

The effect was brilliant and terrifying. It caused panic among the magpins, who were already herded towards the back of the station. They screeched to one another as they zigzagged this way and that, colliding with each other, and they withdrew further and further until they were in the corner of the hallway.

Even the mice were terrified by the Prowler Owl, and they darted in all directions, frantically scuttling into old tin cans or round in circles like tiny clockwork toys.

'Get the net!' shouted Charlie.

The flits swarmed into his rucksack, pulling a mosquito net that belonged to his mum out across the floor.

'Benedict!' cried Edie to get his attention, and each took a corner of the net, throwing it over the magpins, who were cowering in the corner. Then they wrapped them up in it so that they couldn't escape.

For a moment there was an eerie silence.

'That was truly crazeeee!' said Benedict again.

A late-night train rattled past on the northbound side.

Benedict bent down and let the jewellery trickle through his fingers. 'This is some haul.' He took a small notebook out of his pocket and began to make a list, and as he laid each item down the mice scuttled to and fro, moving everything to the signal box for safety.

'Jot?' Impy shouted. 'Are you here?'

There was a muffled reply from the last of the crates on the edge of the semicircle. It was sealed with a lid.

Impy flew over to it and peered through some mesh at the side. 'I can see Jot!' she cried.

'Charlie!' Edie said. 'Help me lift the lid on this crate.'

Together they heaved it off and Edie shone her torch inside. There, huddled together in a circle at the bottom, was a group of about fifty flits blinking in the bright beam of light. Impy and Speckle dropped down beside them, running round the circle, until a flit with a heavily bandaged arm turned and threw her good arm round them, pressing them both to her.

'Flum!' Impy cried. They stayed folded in her good arm, buried in her neck, until Impy lifted her head. 'What happened to your other arm?'

'I broke it when I fell,' said Flum.

'Where's the nut?'

'I . . . I . . . don't know,' said Flum.

Speckle disentangled himself from Flum and hurled himself at a slightly taller flit with a quiff of hair. He hung onto him as if he would never let go. Edie knew that this had to be Jot. She recognised him from the picture. Elfin was down there too, clutching at her reunited family members.

'Everyone should move to the signal box,' Elfin said.

'We can't fly,' said Jot. 'They've put sticky stuff on our wings to stop us from escaping.'

'Where's Nid?' Flum said suddenly.

Edie had been thinking just the same.

'We've not seen him,' said Jot. 'Isn't he with you?'

'He fell from the train this evening. Here at Wilde Street!' cried Impy. 'We thought he'd be here.' She looked despairingly towards the train tracks.

'We haven't seen Nid . . . or the young flits and the unhatched nuts,' Jot said. 'Someone is using them. Training them to steal. We hear the songs they sing, but we don't know where they're being kept.'

At this the birds that were netted in the corner began to cackle and squawk. It was only bird language but it seemed to merge into a series of recognisable screeches.

'Ss-crree-ch! Sss-crree-ch! Ss-cree-EECH!'

'What are they saying?' said Charlie.

'It sounds like "Creech",' said Edie. 'Vera Creech. I thought she had something to do with all this.'

At that moment a ball of feathers hurled itself at the crate from the top of the signal box. It knocked Elfin to the ground and pinned her down with a scaly claw. It was a particularly bold magpin that had escaped the net.

Jot caught the arm of a Vault flit. 'Give me your needle!' he hissed.

The Vault flit whipped it out of his belt and Jot ran towards the bird, prodding the needle hard at the base of the bird's neck until it drew blood.

Elfin rolled herself clear of the bird's claw, but the magpin lashed out at Jot, knocking him backwards. Several of the mice had found a pot of 'wing stick' and the Vault flits started to catapult globules of it at the magpin's wings. It tried to flap them, but the sticky stuff had got into its feathers and was already beginning to harden.

Jot got up and forced the bird backwards, pointing the needle at its throat. He pushed it closer to the edge of the platform. The tracks began their tell-tale clicking to announce that a train was coming, and for the first time the magpin looked nervous as it could no longer fly away. The rattle of the train grew louder.

Jot glanced at the tunnel and the magpin darted to one side and snatched the needle out of his hand. Jot lunged after it, falling to the ground only centimetres from the edge of the platform, and the magpin stood over him, holding a scaly claw over his throat. Edie wanted to kick out at the magpin, but was terrified it would kill Jot if she or Charlie came too close.

'Don't move . . . anyone,' Jot gasped.

The whoosh of air along the platform and the rumble in the tunnel told them all that the train was only seconds away. The ground began to shudder and Edie could feel vibrations running up and down her spine.

'*Let him GO!*' cried a small, high-pitched voice just beyond the magpin, and Speckle flung himself at the magpin's neck, lassoing it with a silver chain from one of the crates. It began to choke the bird, and it twisted round, trying to nip Speckle and flap its sticky wings, but Speckle pulled it back so that it lifted its foot from Jot and staggered closer and closer to the edge of the platform.

The train roared into the station. Clackety-clack! Clackety-clack! *Phwooshm!*

'Spe-ckle!' croaked Jot, every muscle taut with anxiety as he ran to the edge of the platform. 'Speckle!' he cried again. He looked in horror down at the tracks, expecting to see both Speckle and the magpin crushed on the rails, but the train was gone and there was nothing there.

'*Jot!*' the same small voice called out. 'Up here.'

Jot and all the assembled raiders turned to see

Speckle standing on the top of the signal box, still holding the chain.

He flew down beside Jot and the two brothers held each other tight.

'I got him,' he said.

Edie guessed the magpin had been swept up and carried away with the train. But, best of all, Speckle had found his voice.

Chapter Forty

After the loss of the rogue magpin, the birds in the net had fallen silent, their eyes staring through the mesh, round and unblinking. Then one by one they started up their cries of 'Ss-cre-eech! Sss-cree-eech!' again, only less confidently.

Charlie and Benedict went back to secure the net and try to quieten them.

'Is Vera *here*?' said Impy.

'I don't know,' said Edie. 'Something's not right. We still don't know where the young flits are and the unhatched nut babies.'

'And Nid,' said Impy. She looked as if she might cry.

Edie walked down the station platform with Impy, far from all the others, and back towards the passageway that had led them here. She was searching for another tunnel or something that might lead them to Vera Creech. Her eyes drifted downwards and the beam of her head torch caught sight of a small figure bobbing along the platform wall – running, cartwheeling, jumping.

'Nid!' she cried. 'You're safe!'

She rested her hand on the platform and waited for Nid to somersault onto it.

Impy flung her arms round him and then beat her fists on Nid's chest. 'Why did you do that?' she said. 'I thought you were dead! I told you never to ride on top of the trains!'

Nid looked sheepish but proud all at the same time.

'What happened after you fell?' asked Edie.

'I tumbled into the dark, and the clatter of the train's wheels was so roaring loud that I thought I would be sucked under them,' said Nid. 'But then I was blown sideways, whoosh, and landed on the platform. I lay there for a long time trying to get my breath back and the bump was sore. I was scared then in the cold and dark. I called for Jot, but there was only quiet so I set off into that walkway behind me, feeling my way along the wall and –'

Nid was about to carry on when a large bird hopped out of the shadows. It made two more hop-jumps until it was only a metre or so away. It was Shadwell. The spy bird. Nid faltered and Edie could see that, despite his bold jump, the spy bird had really scared him. Shadwell darted forward and snatched him up in his beak, holding him like a splinter caught in a pair of tweezers.

'No!' cried Impy.

Nid's mouth opened and shut in shock but no sound came out. The bird hopped into the shadowy passageway and set off at a lolloping run. There was no time to call the alarm or get the others. Edie knew that whatever happened, she and Impy mustn't let the spy bird out of their sight or they might never see Nid again.

Shadwell turned into a new passageway beyond the stairs that they hadn't seen. Edie followed, with Impy flying just in front of her, as the spy bird ran and hop-jumped ahead of them. Every now and then it would stretch its wings and fly a couple of metres and then resume its hop-jump.

The tunnel twisted and turned away from Wilde Street Station and at one point it split into two. A right turn took them to a siding where the train tracks led to a dead end.

Edie stepped out onto the small platform and gasped. Strings of sparkling lights and jewelled decorations festooned the walls. Silvery paperchains zigzagged this way and that, and mirrored balls twinkled as they caught the light. It was a glittering cave and parked up against the buffers at the end of the platform was an old Tube train carriage painted a deep red with gold lettering on the side. *London Transport.*

On the tracks in front of the carriage were two small flatbed trucks loaded with bars of moulded gold, precious metals and sealed packages, which Edie expected contained jewellery.

That wasn't all. At the far end, balanced on an old workbench, stood a giant painted birthday cake. Its three layers were decorated with elaborate baubles and gold leaf, and a huge candlestick sat on top. It was as if Edie and Impy had stumbled into a palace grotto.

A strange fiery glow shone at the windows of the train and the spy bird hopped through the doors with Nid. Edie and Impy ran to a window and saw Vera bent over a furnace pot wearing goggles, gloves and a large apron, and she was feeding it with the spoils of her pickpocketing. Her back was stooped and her face was drawn in concentration as she tipped the molten metal into a mould.

When she saw Shadwell she lifted her goggles and took

off her gloves. The spy bird hopped onto her shoulder and dropped Nid onto her flattened hand and she closed her fist round him and pressed her eyeglass to her face.

Edie rushed into the carriage with Impy hidden in her plait. 'Let him go!' she said.

Vera Creech turned. The eyeglass dropped. 'So, you found me, you wretch.'

The carriage was hot and felt over-bright. Most of the seats had been taken out and behind Vera was a long workbench. A lamp on a metal arm was angled over the top and a rack of tools held tiny pliers, tweezers and a soldering iron. Across the worktop were scattered pieces of broken jewellery, rings with precious stones and watch cogs and springs. Dozens of tiny figures were bent over their work – separating gemstones into piles – rubies, emeralds, pearls, chips of jade and diamonds. Some polished the items to a shine, while others were making new jewellery out of old. One flit was crafting tiny seed pearls and gemstones into flowers and filigree leaves to decorate a gold birdcage, and the jewelled bird from the pendant that Edie had spotted round Vera Creech's neck was inside it.

'Those are young flits,' Impy whispered. 'She's got them working for her.'

A figure bobbed out from behind the tool rack and ran up and down, scattering watch cogs and gemstones. He was clutching a boiled sweet.

'It's Bead!' whispered Impy sharply. 'Miss Creech's pet!'

Bead looked appalled when he saw them. 'What are you *doing* here?' he whispered nervously. 'She won't like it!'

'Get back to work, Bead!' said Vera.

'Yes, everybody, come along. Come along!' He clapped his hands together and turned on the big lamp. Vera lifted up the delicate birdcage and held it out to Edie.

'Go on,' she said. 'Why don't you look? You were curious enough to poke around my office. Shadwell told me.'

Edie took the birdcage. It *was* beautiful. Delicate leaves and fruits that the flits had crafted were twisted round the cage bars like vines, and the songbird inside was made of silver and studded with green emeralds. Vera Creech turned a crank at the base of the cage and the bird sang a single mournful high note that descended into a cascade of watery trills. Edie was for a moment enchanted. She reached out her hand to open the cage and take out the bird.

'Don't touch the bird!' shouted Vera. 'It's not for you to play with. It's a present for *me*! It's my party and I didn't invite you. I knew you'd spoil everything.'

Edie snatched back her hand. Any sense of enchantment vanished. Now the whole place was beginning to feel suffocating.

Chapter
Forty-One

Wilde Street

Bead prodded at the young flits to keep them busy and clapped his hands. A chorus of voices started up. '*Pick-ing pockets, lit-tle fingers, stealing is the only way.*'

'Stealing is against every Flit Forager Code,' shouted Impy. 'You shouldn't work for her.'

The young flits looked at her curiously.

Vera ignored Impy and, adjusting her eyeglass, merely watched as they took everything in. Then she held Nid up to yet another cage that was dangling over their heads. It was lined with fine netting and inside were several more baby flits and a pile of unhatched nuts. She opened the door and threw Nid inside. This must be the nursery, Edie thought, and as soon as the flits hatched they were set to work.

Impy buried her head in Edie's hair. 'This is awful!'

Vera had once again raised her eyeglass to her face. 'Get her too,' she said in a bored voice. Shadwell landed on Edie's head, snatching at her hair until he had Impy caught in his beak. Edie whirled round and grabbed at Shadwell, but he hovered just out of reach and then flew upwards to toss Impy in the cage with Nid.

'Give them back!' shouted Edie angrily.

'No,' said Vera.

'Why are you doing all this?'

'You think that stupid job in the Lost Property Office is what I do?' she replied. 'Yes, I *find* things . . . but I don't just give them back.' She pointed at the trucks laden with bars of precious metals and bags of gemstones. 'I make them better and give them to other people who aren't so careless.'

'Sell them you mean?' said Edie.

'You could say that, but I think we can still refer to them as "lost" and "found".'

'But nothing here is *yours*. You are stealing things to melt down and change and –' Edie looked at the painted birthday cake, which at a closer view she could see was made of papier mâché. 'Why's that here?'

'B-because . . .' Vera's cool confidence faltered. Then she recovered herself. 'I have every right to have a beautiful birthday just like everyone else, and this is *my* cake and *my* decorations and *my* presents.' She sounded like an angry child. 'It's *my* special day!'

'What do you mean?' asked Edie. 'If it's your birthday, we could have had tea at the Lost Property Office with chocolate mini rolls and paper hats.'

'Your father', said Vera, 'is kind. Mine was not. He didn't make my birthdays "normal". He never let me celebrate birthdays or Christmas. No presents, no cakes, no treats. No friends.'

Edie didn't know what to say. It sounded weird. Why would Vera want everything now that she didn't have as a child? She looked at the eyeglass hanging round Vera's neck. 'And where did you get that?'

Vera leant in very close to Edie's face so that her eye was magnified into a hard-boiled egg. 'I know you see them too, Edie,' she said. 'I saw so many little creatures as a child. They were the only people I felt I could talk to. Them and the birds. The birds listened to me, and still do, but I was in despair when I grew up and the little creatures faded away. Then, in my first week at the Lost Property Office, I found this eyeglass in one of the sacks.'

'And you never reported it? What if someone had come to find it?' Edie said, wondering who the owner of the eyeglass was.

'I didn't think it was anything special and then a few days later on my way home I realised that it could show me things. I saw Bead trying to steal my food and another little creature running across a ticket hall and I realised I could see them again! And it made me so happy.' She started to cry. 'I was so lonely, Edie.'

Edie felt confused.

'I think you understand, Edie. After all, you took that box from the Storeroom at the End . . .'

Edie burnt with the truth of this. As Vera sniffed and dabbed at her eyes she stretched out her hand towards her.

'Edie!' Impy called out from the cage. 'Look down there.'

Edie looked over to where Impy was pointing. There was another box on the table beside Vera. It was wooden and not unlike her own flit box but larger and more robust with tiny holes drilled in the top. The lid was stamped: *Fragile. Live Creatures in Transit. Trade.*

'What's that?' she said.

'It's a travelling box,' said Vera, sniffling. 'For the little creatures.'

Edie leant over and lifted the lid. Inside were layers of wire netting.

'Where are you taking them?' Edie asked slowly, her sympathy for Vera evaporating. Juniper was one thing, but she sensed this was much, much worse.

'They're going to a new home where they'll be put in a nice glass case.'

There was a terrible silence as Edie realised what the box meant. Despite the fiery furnace, the carriage felt strangely chilly. 'You're going to sell them too?'

Vera's face narrowed and her sniffling stopped like a tap that had been switched off.

'Of course. There are collectors out there – no questions asked.'

Edie paused to marshall her thoughts. So there might be other adults who could see the flits? And want to collect them? She thought of the tiny running figure tooled on the leather eyeglass pouch.

'You never *cared* about them *at all*,' said Edie. 'You just realised that you could *use* them. You stole the youngest flits to turn them into pickpockets and now you're going to sell them too. *None* of this belongs to you: *not* the gold, *not* the jewellery and *NOT* the flits.'

Impy and Nid gave a little cheer from the cage overhead.

'You're right. I don't care about *any* of that. After my birthday is over everything will be sold. You have to take what you want in life.'

There was a short silence.

'But no one has birthdays like this!' Edie shouted. 'Sending presents to themselves. Sitting alone with a huge stupid over-the-top cake. You only feel good when you're *using* other people. Making them feel small.' Inside she felt the same hot, difficult feelings that she had felt at school with Linny.

'Temper!' said Vera calmly. 'Perhaps, Edie, you would like to help me instead of whining? It can be our secret. You can spend my birthday with me,' she wheedled.

'Not when it's like this!' Edie picked up the delicate birdcage. 'You must give all this back!'

'No . . . I can't,' said Vera, and she snatched at the cage, but Edie held on. They tussled back and forth until the birdcage dropped to the floor and broke.

All the flits stopped working and Bead gave a strangled gasp.

When Vera Creech spoke it was in a very cold, quiet voice. 'You have spoken out of turn and you have broken my present. Now I shall set the magpins on you.'

'You mean those birds? I suppose you trap them too. Make them do what you want?'

'I'm clever with birds. I discovered that when I was younger too. I know how to train them.'

'Well, the magpins won't come now,' said Edie.

'What do you mean?' Vera drew back. 'What have you done with them?'

'We've trapped them,' said Edie. 'They can't escape.'

Vera snapped her fingers and Shadwell flew at Edie, pulling at her plaits so that Edie backed away towards the front of the train carriage. Vera opened the door to the old driver's cab and pushed her hard, so that Edie stumbled backwards into the cab, and then she slammed the door shut and locked it.

Chapter Forty-Two

Wilde Street

Edie leant her head against the door. She was trapped and she was on her own. She knew she had to get a message to Charlie and Benedict, and she realised how foolish it had been to come here alone with Impy. She was sure the others would be looking for them, but there were so many tunnels and passageways. She tried to open the window but apart from a small gap at the top it was stuck fast.

The trucks waiting on the tracks were a horrible reminder of Vera Creech's plans. Edie sat down heavily on the driver's seat.

'Psst!'

Something had fluttered down onto her hair and was tugging gently at her plait.

'Impy! How did you escape?'

Impy held up a tiny pocket knife. 'Nid had this hidden in his bag and I cut a hole in the mesh and crawled through.' She pointed up at a small pipe that connected the cabin to the carriage. 'I can go and find Charlie and Benedict.'

'It's too dangerous,' said Edie. 'How will you find your way? And if the spy bird was to realise you'd gone . . .' That didn't bear thinking about.

A sharp tap made them both look up. The spy bird was at the window peering in.

'Hide!' whispered Edie, but it was too late. Shadwell had seen Impy and his eye swivelled round as he cocked his head to one side. He tapped again at the glass and poked his sharp beak through the gap in the window.

'What are we going to do?' whispered Impy.

'We have to send a sign somehow to the others to let them know where we are.'

The spy bird watched them for another moment or two and then hopped back round to the train carriage. Edie knew he was going to get Vera.

'Quick, Impy! We have to think of something!'

Impy had flitted down onto the dashboard of the train and was studying the levers and buttons. 'Can we make it move?' said Impy.

Edie lifted the driver's handle to the left and right and

pulled at the brake lever, but she had no idea how to start and drive a Tube train.

Impy flew up above Edie's head. 'What about this?' she said. She was pointing to what looked like an old school bell high up on the wall. The driver's cab had been fitted with some kind of alarm and it had a crank handle underneath. That was it! If they could sound the train's alarm the others might hear it. Edie stood up on the chair and took hold of the handle. She tugged hard but it was stiff and rusty and only moved a fraction. The bell remained silent.

'Come ON,' said Edie, tugging it again.

'Here!' said Impy. She held out a tiny blue bottle. 'It's lavender oil. I like to carry it with me. It's an F7 thing.'

'Hurry!' said Edie as Impy flew up and tipped two tiny drops of oil onto the crank handle. Edie tugged again and the crank began to move as the oil seeped into the mechanism. As she turned it, the bell began to ring. Faster and faster she turned it until – *Brrrrrrrinnnnnng!* – a long trilling, joyful note sounded and filled the air.

Edie turned the crank handle again. The bell sound became a brassy fanfare that filled the station and soared into the tunnels. Edie and Impy laughed as they could barely hear themselves think. It was fantastically, wonderfully, ear-shatteringly loud.

There was pandemonium behind them. The spy bird

shot into the air and Vera came rushing out of the carriage with her hands over her ears.

'Stop that noise!' she cried, banging on the door of the cab. The eyeglass swung from her neck.

Edie turned the bell crank again. 'Get the key from her pocket,' she cried to Impy.

Impy slipped through the gap in the window and Edie could see her bobbing about behind Vera, trying to slip into her pocket. Within seconds she had tugged it out and was back at the window of the cab with the key in her arms, unnoticed by Shadwell. She thrust it at Edie.

'Can you go and free the other flits?' said Edie.

Impy disappeared back through the pipe that led to the main carriage just as Vera started rattling the handle. 'Where's the key? Shadwell! Find my key.'

Edie gave one last ring of the bell and at last Charlie and Benedict appeared in the entrance to the siding followed by Flum, Jot and Speckle and a cavalry of mice. They all stopped in their tracks when they saw the old carriage, the freight trucks loaded with booty and the strange birthday grotto.

Edie stood up and banged on the driver's cab and Charlie came running over. 'You're here!' he said. 'That bell was crazy. What is this place?'

'Edie! Thank goodness you're all right!' said Benedict. 'We've been looking for you everywhere.'

Edie unlocked the door of the cab. 'Quick,' she said. 'Catch Vera.' Unnoticed, Vera Creech had run over to the trucks and was now releasing the brakes on the first one. They started to roll down the tracks and Vera ran alongside.

Benedict ran towards her, trying to catch hold of her coat. 'Miss Creech . . . Vera . . . come back!' cried Benedict.

'Never,' she said, and she scrambled up onto the second truck as it gathered speed.

Benedict ran after her, trying to keep up, but Shadwell swooped low across his face, blinding him for a moment, and he stumbled and fell.

Vera stood waving at them with Shadwell on her shoulder as the trucks gathered speed and disappeared round a bend in the tunnel.

Charlie and Edie helped Benedict to his feet. 'Come on. We should go after her.'

'NO!' cried Benedict for the second time that night. 'We don't know where these tracks connect with the main line and there might be an electric rail. It's too dangerous, Edie. She probably knows these tunnels and passageways like the back of her hand.'

'We can't let her get away!'

'Let's just think, Edie. There must be another way.'

Edie looked back to the carriage where all the flits were. There was someone else who could help them.

'Wait here,' she said.

Chapter Forty-Three

Wilde Street

'**B**ead?' Edie cried as she jumped back into the carriage.

Nid and Impy had set up a zipwire to bring all the baby flits down from the nursery cage and Flum and Speckle and the mice had formed an assembly line to collect all the unhatched nuts.

'Where's Bead?'

Bead emerged from behind a soldering iron, trembling and clutching a boiled sweet. He looked behind Edie, expecting Vera Creech to reappear with her eyeglass.

'Vera's gone, Bead. She's left you behind,' Edie said.

'Left me behind?' he said, wrapping his arms more tightly round the sweet.

'You can come with us, but first you have to tell us where those trucks go.'

Bead ducked back down behind the soldering iron. 'I can't!'

'You'll be on your own again if you don't help us. Vera Creech didn't care about you. She'd probably have sold you to some collector who might pin you down like a butterfly in a cabinet. And you'd have no sugar!'

Bead's head peered round again. 'On my own? No sugar?'

'No,' said Edie firmly.

'And you'll take me with you?'

'Yes, we will,' said Edie more kindly.

'Well . . .' he said slowly and then the rest tumbled out. 'There's a maintenance train that comes along the Bakerloo Line every night and she attaches the trucks to it. It goes all the way to the depot where the freight trains are.'

'Of course!' said Charlie. 'She's clever! The freight trains are just like a giant delivery service to her.'

'This is just a siding,' said Bead. 'Just round the next bend the track joins with the main line.'

'When does the maintenance train come?' Charlie asked.

'I think it comes at one-thirty in the morning,' said Bead. 'She sends the trucks down around this time and waits with them.'

'That's in fifteen minutes,' said Charlie, looking at his watch.

Edie helped Flum and Speckle to get all the flits safely into her rucksack and hoisted it onto her back. 'These tracks lead down to the main train line,' Edie called out to Benedict. 'We have to go back to Wilde Street Station.'

'How do you know?' said Benedict.

'You probably wouldn't believe me if I told you!' cried Edie, waving at him to follow as the mice led the way and she, Charlie and Benedict ran at full tilt behind them.

In the distance there was a sudden chorus of screechy cries as if blown towards them on a gust of wind.

'I thought the magpins were trapped in the net,' said Edie.

'They are,' said Charlie. 'At least, they were.' Edie could tell by the tone of his voice that he was no longer convinced.

They turned their torches off as they neared the end of the passageway, as they could once again see the glow from the magpins' camp, and felt their way along the wall and out to the middle of the platform. It seemed days, weeks even, since they had first stepped out here, and yet it was little over an hour ago.

Elfin and Jot bobbed up out of the gloom.

'She's got the magpins!' Jot said. 'We tried to stop her, but she carried the whole net away with her.'

'Where?' said Charlie.

'We flew after her but she disappeared down there.' Elfin pointed to the far end of the platform.

'What's happened?' said Benedict, oblivious to Elfin and Jot.

'Vera's taken the magpins,' said Edie. Almost on cue they heard another chorus of screechy cries reverberating around the tunnel walls.

'Let's just wait for the maintenance train,' said Edie. 'She has to come out then. The tunnel that led from the siding must connect with the main line down there somewhere.' Charlie flicked on his torch again and, for a brief moment, shone the beam along the main line. In the shadows beyond the mouth of the tunnel they could just make out a second tunnel branching off to the left with its own line of track.

'That must be it,' he whispered, turning off the torch and allowing them to be folded into the gloom once again.

They crouched in silence. Somewhere water dripped. It was spooky and the damp felt as if it was crawling into Edie's bones. She imagined Vera Creech waiting too with her trucks.

Charlie spoke first. 'What's that?'

Edie could feel under her feet the low thrum of a vibration. It was different to the Tube train sound, heavier and deeper, as if a creature were coming out of the earth. The tracks began to clink and rattle as a warning that a vehicle was on the line and it rumbled in the tunnels like distant thunder.

'It must be the maintenance train,' whispered Charlie.

'Wait!' said Benedict, drawing them back into the passageway.

The thunder grew louder and filled the tunnel, and as it came nearer there was the sound of heavy metal chains clanking.

A single bright headlamp swung into view and lit up the whole station, and a huge yellow engine emerged slowly out of the tunnel like an ungainly elephant. Behind it came a convoy of flat-bed wagons carrying skips filled with gravel, concrete railway sleepers, drums with rolls of cable and bags of cement. The noise was deafening as the convoy drove through Wilde Street at a snail's pace. From the passageway they watched as the driver's cab slowly clattered past, followed by a convoy of wagons.

'Look!' said Edie.

Out of the side tunnel came Vera's two trucks. She had hooked them to the last wagon with a rope and she stood on the first truck like a charioteer as she was pulled along. Pinned beside her on the truck was the net of magpins and the noise of the maintenance train made them squawk with alarm. There was no sign of Shadwell.

'We have to unhitch her,' shouted Benedict, and he jumped out and ran alongside the maintenance train until he was able to leap onto the flat-bed wagon in front of her. He threw an empty sack from a pile on the wagon and a roll of rope down to Edie and Charlie as they jogged alongside.

Vera gave a shriek when she saw Benedict and, leaning forward, she swiped at him as he bent down to grapple with the looped rope but he was just out of reach.

'No-oo!' cried Vera, stuffing some of the booty into her pockets. 'Look! You can have what's left. Please, just let me go. I can board a ship at Harwich and . . . disappear.'

Just for a moment Edie wanted to let her go. Maybe disappearing would be the best thing. Edie had said what she wanted to say to Vera and thought of the sad cardboard birthday cake. 'Shouldn't we give her a chance?' she called out above the noise.

'She stole all that stuff, Edie!' cried Charlie.

'What about the travelling box for the "little creatures"!' said Impy and, dragging Nid after her, she flew past Edie towards Vera's trucks.

Edie's sympathy evaporated. 'I want the eyeglass!' she called to Vera.

Vera clutched at it, realising it was up for bargaining. 'Only if you let me go.'

Edie said nothing. She realised that Charlie had left

her side and was sprinting back up the platform.

'I've almost untied it,' shouted Benedict as he pulled at the rope.

'Take it!' said Vera, a note of panic creeping into her voice. She unlooped the eyeglass from her neck and, stuffing it in its leather pouch, she threw it to the ground beside Edie. There was a muffled tinkle of glass inside the pouch. 'Now let me go!'

'Never!' said Benedict, just as Vera had cried out to *him* earlier.

The magpins were becoming more restless and pressed up against the net in a tight ball.

Benedict loosened the last twist of rope that connected the trucks to the train and, straining with his fingers, he unhitched it. The trucks with all their stolen booty slowly ground to a halt.

Vera gave a wild shriek and tried to launch herself past Benedict and across onto the maintenance train, but Impy and Nid had secretly tied her shoelaces together. Instead she tripped and fell sideways and her feet became tangled in the magpin net. The magpins complained furiously as Vera tried to free herself. She pulled one foot free of the netting, but as she did so she ripped a hole in it and one by one the magpins slipped through, screeching and flapping around her head in a whirling mass.

'Stop this at once,' she cried at the birds, but they

refused to listen. They were distracted by the sight of the Prowler Owl with its headlight eyes making its way slowly down the platform on a skateboard. It stopped and gave a loud megaphone hoot.

'Attack them!' Vera cried again to the magpins, but they were now swooping up and down the station and screeching in alarm like paper planes blown about in a gale.

Vera, having freed both her feet, leapt down onto the platform in a bid to escape, but Edie jumped on top of her, and Benedict, scrambling down from the maintenance train, ran back along the platform to help her. Together they covered Vera with the huge sack and tied rope around her arms and legs as if she were an awkward parcel. Only her head stuck out of the top with its tuft of blue-streaked hair.

'You useless creatures,' Vera cried out in frustration to the magpins. 'Attack them, I say!' But the magpins were no longer listening to her commands. The Prowler Owl, operated by Charlie, was still trundling up and down and they could see Vera was trapped. Their beaks no longer appeared to be sneering and crocodile-like. Instead they just looked terrified.

Edie turned her attention to the flits, wondering where they were.

'Down here!' cried Impy, landing on the ground

beside the eyeglass. She called to Nid and Jot to help her and they dragged the pouch towards the train tracks.

'I'm going to make sure it's destroyed for good.' But just as they reached the edge of the platform, ready to tip it over, a black form swooped down and snatched it from them. Shadwell!

'Help me, Shadwell!'cried Vera, but Shadwell swept away from her and with a defiant cry of 'kraaa' he called to the magpins and, wheeling round, flew after the maintenance train. The magpins immediately stopped their screeching and gathered in formation behind him. As the flat-bed wagons disappeared one by one into the tunnel, the magpins went after them and Shadwell dropped down and perched on the last wagon as it entered the tunnel with the eyeglass pouch under one claw.

'Shadwell! Come back!' called Vera into the darkness, but Shadwell had vanished and her sack-like body slumped to the platform.

The whole episode had only taken minutes, as long as it had taken the maintenance train to crawl slowly through the station, but it felt to Edie that it had lasted all night. Now there was an eerie silence and the platform was gloomy and dark once again.

Benedict stood over her. 'Wilde Street is now officially a crime scene,' he said. 'We need to call the police and get these trucks off the main line before the Tube trains start up at five-thirty. I'll have to go back to the office and make the calls where I can get a signal. Will you be all right, Edie, staying here with Charlie to watch Vera?'

Edie nodded and went to fetch the bike lamps from the hallway so that they would have more light as they waited, and the flits went with her to prepare for the journey home. Charlie took off his Prowler Owl outfit and stood guard over Vera.

'You have spoilt everything,' Vera said again when Edie returned. 'My magpins have gone and Shadwell has escaped with the eyeglass.'

'I heard the glass break,' said Edie, hanging a bike lamp from a bench. 'And I hope it is broken. No one should be able to see the flits after their thirteenth birthday. It's all wrong.'

At this Vera looked awkward and unhappy.

'Who were you sending all that stuff to?' Charlie asked.

But Vera refused to say anything more at all.

Impy appeared, hovering in front of Edie's nose.

'We're ready,' she said.

*

Edie returned once again to the hallway and, opening the top of her rucksack, she peeped inside. Nestled on top of her cape was Impy's family – Flum, Nid, Speckle and Jot, and their nut. Ranged around them in groups were numerous other flits, many of them clutching a nut. The young 'pickpocket' flits were asleep in Benedict's bobble hat and Bead sat cross-legged on her glove, sucking on a Polo mint.

Edie folded her arms around the rucksack – she now had a vast extended family to look after, a cargo that to her was far more precious than all the jewellery.

Chapter Forty-Four

Wilde Street to **Alexandra Park Road**

I t was a long night.

Benedict returned with several police officers and London Underground officials. They set up arc lights and marvelled at the contents of the trucks and the crates and were completely baffled by the number of cherry stones. The trucks were returned to the sidings before the Tube trains started again at 5.30 a.m. and Vera was handcuffed and taken into custody at a police station in Baker Street. More officials were called in to examine Vera's train carriage and were even more baffled by the paper chains and the birthday cake. A woman from the RSPB came to investigate the descriptions Edie had given the officials of a rogue crow and a flock of magpins, but there was no sign of the birds and no reports of them emerging at the end of a train line. They had completely vanished.

Both Vera and Benedict had a lot of questions to answer.

As Edie and Charlie left Wilde Street for the last time they went to say goodbye to Elfin. The mice had disappeared into the gaps and cracks that lined the platform walls, into a subterranean world of their own, but Elfin and the Vault flits, now reunited with their families, sat on the roof of the signal box waiting for the first train back to Waterloo.

'We won't forget what you did for Jot,' said Edie.

Jot's head appeared through the zip of the rucksack. 'Come and see us when we get back to the Hillside Camp.'

'Might do,' said Elfin, wiping smut from her face, but she gave him a crooked half-smile. Then she flew up and handed Jot her needle. 'It's yours. You might have saved my life, remember!'

Jot turned pink with pride and ducked out of sight.

*

The sky was turning a pale milky pink by the time they eventually reached Alexandra Park Road. Benedict and Charlie disappeared into the kitchen to make pancakes.

Edie carried her rucksack upstairs to settle the now very extended family of flits in the box. They filled every corner, jumping on and off the cork stools as if they were miniature trampolines, taking baths in the anchovy tin and rolling themselves up in the jewel-coloured duvets.

She found some cotton buds and vinegar and helped the older flits to clean the wing stick off their wings. They shook them out and flapped them, rising up into the air as they tested them out. Giddy with freedom after the long days spent as prisoners, the younger flits explored Edie's room, pulling things out of her pencil case, tangling the wires of her headphones, and tipping over her bead box so that they could chase the beads as they scattered across the floor.

Jot led a needle-throwing competition and Nid built a skateboard ramp out of Edie's geometry set. Bead sat apart from the other flits in a jam jar on Edie's shelf, watching.

In an attempt to keep order Edie prepared a feast. She filled a row of egg cups and bottle tops with raisins and cereal hoops and tiny squares of apple and sneaked the entire pot of chocolate spread out of the kitchen. For a while there was silence as they all ate.

Impy hopped up onto her hand. 'Can we go home now?' she said.

Edie knew this was coming. Only for a brief few seconds had she imagined that they might want to stay here with her as the extended family she had always wanted. But it would never work. Fifty flits wouldn't last long with only one box for space. Her bedroom already looked a mess and they would spill out into the house, teasing Bilbo and causing havoc. For every one Nid there were now three or four younger flits who were just as reckless and energetic, needing space to tumble and jump. There were numerous Jots and Impys who would want to go out foraging and exploring, and Flums and Speckles who would want to create their own homes again, all ready for more nuts to hatch. Most of all they weren't pets and they didn't belong to Edie. Fierce, determined, independent Impy had taught her that. Of course they would want to go home.

'Yes,' Edie said.

Tonight after school she and Charlie would return them all to the Hillside Camp to begin rebuilding their home. But she also had another problem. She held up the jam jar with Bead inside.

'Do you want to go home too, Bead, back to Tilbury?'

'No. I want to stay here in London.'

'But you can't live with these flits after what you've done.'

Bead looked down at his shoes.

'There is a girl I know who is looking for someone like you to work for her,' Edie said.

'What would I have to do?' said Bead.

'You'd have to act a bit and dress up as a pixie!'

'That's all right,' said Bead. 'I like pixies.'

'And you might have to change your name to Goatsbeard.'

'Well, I was never that fond of Bead, so Goatsbeard will do just fine.' His eyes narrowed. 'Would the girl give me sugar?'

'Yes. I think she would.'

Edie found a large padded envelope and Bead made himself comfortable inside with a large boiled sweet. She addressed the envelope to Juniper and gave it to Benedict to deliver to Ada's shop first thing the next morning. On the back she wrote: *Feed me sweet things.*

Ada, back from her trip away with Baby Sol, could hand-deliver it to Juniper.

*

It wasn't long before @JunipBerry began posting again on Instagram. She captioned her first photo: *Live pixie show!*

There, sat on a mossy bank, Edie saw Bead wearing a pixie outfit and a pointed red hat. He might have looked really dismal in his new home except for the large stick of pink rock that lay on its side under his feet. He was dipping a finger into the pink stickiness and positively beaming. The comments that followed were much as before:

Aaaah! SOOO sweet.

Is that for real?

You are weird, @JunipBerry!

To which Juniper replied: *Seeing is believing.*

Chapter Forty-Five

Alexandra Park Road

'We're home!' shouted Dad from the hallway. Edie burst out of the kitchen, stumbling over the bags and clinging first to Dad and then pushing past him to find Mum.

Heta stood wrapped in a snow coat and boots and clutching a loaf of dark rye bread. Edie pressed her face into Mum's neck, smelling the scent of pine and rye.

'I'm glad you're back, Mum.'

'So am I, Edie. And I've brought Gran with me.'

There on the path, wrapped in a blanket and sitting in a wheelchair, was Granny Agata with her leg in plaster. She looked as if she was made of bone china – much more frail than Edie remembered, but her eyes were bright blue. She held out her arms towards Edie. Two crooked branches on a winter tree.

Mum pulled off her coat and sat on the bottom step of the stairs so that she could take off her boots.

'I have something for you, Edie,' she said and she dipped her hand into her bag and pulled out a small brown envelope. Edie lifted the flap and inside was a tiny silver goose on a chain. Its neck was outstretched and its wings were open as if it were mid-flight. It was beautiful.

'I've got something for you too, Mum.' She reached into her pocket and brought out the gold ring that Nid had found.

Mum stared at it. 'My wedding ring! Where did you find that, Edie? I lost it years ago when we moved in.' She joyfully slipped it back on her finger.

'I-I . . . It just appeared one day . . . when I was sweeping up in the kitchen.'

Mum held up her hand. The ring still fitted perfectly. She showed Granny Agata.

'It's the house elves, Heta,' Granny Agata said. 'The *kotitonttu.*'

'Mum told me about them,' Edie said.

'In Finland lots of families have house elves,' said Granny Agata. 'I had Tomi and Ulla. Tomi was helpful but Ulla stole buttons.'

'Mum!' said Edie. 'You never told me that.'

'She forgot she ever saw them,' Granny Agata whispered to Edie.

'Well, we don't have house elves here!' said Mum. 'Only Edie's sharp eyes.'

In the kitchen Benedict was already showing Dad the newspaper cuttings and the weblinks to news reports, and he was telling him how the last two days had been 'crazee'.

The Wilde Street Hoard (as it had become known) had caused a huge stir and the *London Herald*, among other newspapers, carried the headlines: *Is this the world's best lost property office?* and *Is Vera Creech London's most successful pickpocket?* Several photos showed Vera looking tight-lipped in custody as she waited for her court case. She refused to tell the police anything about the secret tunnels or her collaborators and, much to Edie's and Charlie's relief, nothing about the flits.

A huge safe had been installed at the Lost Property Office until every item had been reunited with its owner, and as one piece after another was repatriated, journalists began to mill around Baker Street with microphones and cameras.

Grateful owners praised the Lost Property Office, with two of them pledging large sums of money. Dad couldn't believe it when he saw Ursula clutching a cheque and shaking the hand of a jewellery collector in Mayfair. She also wrote a long and apologetic letter to Dad offering him his old job back, praising him for how well he had trained Benedict and his 'delightful' daughter Edie, and she regretted underestimating his managerial abilities. Vera, she said, 'was a bad egg'.

To celebrate, Benedict wore a T-shirt with the slogan: *Small Is the New Big.*

Edie was worried that the magpins and Shadwell might return, but the days passed and there was no sign of them. Without Vera they had no one to answer to and she liked to think of them enjoying their freedom. She told herself that the eyeglass was broken and unuseable.

Edie missed the flits dreadfully, but it wasn't the same kind of painful ache that she felt when Juniper had stolen them. She knew they were busy rebuilding their home and that she could visit them if she wanted to. She hung a tiny lizard charm (that Nid had given her on the day he went home) on the same chain as the silver goose from Finland and wore it under her school uniform. Its tiny jingle was a reminder of all things small. The flit box now felt empty and unused, but Edie showed it to Granny Agata, who stared at it for some time, picking up small pieces of furniture one by one and laying the miniature skateboard 'sofa' on the palm of her crooked hand.

Chapter Forty-Six

Alexandra Park Road to **Highgate**

In the week before Christmas Edie asked Mum if she could take Granny Agata out in her wheelchair. She had invited Charlie over to help her.

'We're taking her to see the Christmas lights,' Edie said, packing a thick blanket.

They took the bus from Alexandra Palace, asking the driver to lower the ramp so that they could push Granny Agata on board. It was packed with Christmas shoppers. As the bus slowly climbed the hill up towards Highgate Station, Edie felt a tap on her shoulder. She turned round and it was Naz. Edie instinctively looked beyond her towards the back of the bus expecting to see the sarcastic faces of Linny and the other girls.

'It's all right. They're not here,' said Naz. 'It's just me.'

She was wearing a plain hoodie and trainers, and the spangled top she had worn at the beginning of Year Seven to copy Linny had disappeared.

'Where are you going?' said Naz.

'Just to see some Christmas lights,' said Edie. She tried to sound casual and disinterested, but her voice felt tight and small again.

'Sounds brilliant,' said Naz.

'Why don't you come with us?' said Granny Agata.

Edie stared at her grandmother. The last thing she wanted was someone from school coming along, someone who she couldn't yet be certain wouldn't spread mean stories about her and make her life a misery.

'OK. Thanks. I'd like that,' said Naz.

Edie looked down.

'Well, that's good, isn't it, Edie?' said Granny Agata.

'So where *is* Linny?' Edie asked.

'Don't know,' said Naz. 'We don't really see each other outside school.'

'Why not?' said Edie. She tried to keep the surprise out of her voice.

'I realised that I didn't really like her any more.'

'And the other girls?'

'I never really liked them in the first place. I want *us* to be friends again, Edie. I tried to tell you earlier, but you didn't want to know.'

Edie knew this was true. She had been so preoccupied with Impy and the flits that there hadn't been room for Naz too.

*

They pushed the wheelchair down the hill from the Highgate Road to the station car park.

'Where are we going?' said Naz.

Edie said nothing and just concentrated on pushing the wheelchair between the gap in the hedge and through the undergrowth, wrestling with it as the dry winter sticks caught in the wheels. They heaved it through into the open space, their breath frosting up in the chilly afternoon air. A startled bird suddenly darted out of a bush in front of them. Edie jumped, casting around to see if Shadwell was perched on a rooftop nearby, but the rooftops were deserted and the bird was only small and frightened like any ordinary London bird would be.

The street lights up on the Highgate Road lit up the old station in front of them. It was still completely intact, like a giant-sized model station on a Hornby railway set.

'What a fabulous secret place, Edie,' said Granny Agata.

'It's amazing!' said Naz. 'A whole station hidden away like this.'

Charlie and Edie managed to manoeuvre Granny Agata up onto the platform and wheel her along its smooth surface to the north end.

'Wait here with Gran,' said Edie to Naz. 'I promise we won't be long.' She and Charlie dropped down into the spiky winter brambles that covered the old track bed and pushed their way through to the huge north wall that supported the old tunnels.

Edie took a few steps towards the bank – the Hillside Camp. For a moment she couldn't see anything. It seemed to be in darkness. A bubble of panic rose up inside her. Perhaps the magpins had returned, or the flits had deserted the camp?

'Impy . . . ? Nid? It's us . . . Edie and Charlie.'

Still nothing, and then one by one tiny pinpricks of light appeared and began to move around, zigzagging here and there. Edie felt a fluttering in front of her nose, followed by a sharp tug on her ear lobe.

'Impy!'

Edie lifted her hand up to her ear and felt Impy step onto it and wrap her arms round her thumb. 'I thought you'd never come.'

Then she called into the darkness, 'All clear!' and pulled at Edie's thumb to lead her forward.

Edie and Charlie followed her and the bank lit up in front of them. A long string of lights fastened between two aluminium cans hung over the terraces, revealing rows of patched-up and restored houses. New walls had been constructed out of packaging and juice cartons, beams from lolly sticks, roofs from old teacups and rubber shoe soles, and one entire house was made from a family-size Marmite pot lying on its side.

The flits gathered on the walkways or appeared in windows and doorways.

Impy tugged at her thumb and led her to a house at the end of one of the terraces. The front was covered by a square of canvas and strung with paper clips and Impy drew it back.

Nid jumped up and cartwheeled towards them and Jot and Speckle showed them Elfin's needle proudly displayed on the wall. Flum was perched alongside the wooden doll's-house cradle Edie had bought from Ada's charity shop. The cradle emitted a high-pitched wail.

Edie's hand flew to her mouth. 'Of course.'

Inside the cradle, on a bed of cotton wool, was a tiny flit – its hair a miniscule tuft of fluff, its legs and arms like pins and its wings folded against its back. It was perfect.

'The nut hatched!' said Edie.

'A week ago!' said Impy. 'And it's a girl.'

'What's she called?' asked Edie.

'Peanut. Pea for short.'

Edie led the way back to the station platform with her hands cupped in front of her. 'I've got something to show you.'

Naz looked puzzled, but Granny Agata sat up expectantly as Edie unfolded her hands. Charlie angled the torch so that they could see what was inside and revealed the flits – all five of them with the cradle.

'This is my Granny Agata and my friend, Naz.'

There was complete silence for a moment as Naz and Granny Agata stared at them. No one moved, and then Impy stood up.

'Hello.'

Naz let out a little scream. Nid, keen not to miss out on the opportunity for a show, sprinted across Edie's hand and cartwheeled up and down her arm.

Granny Agata laughed and clapped her hands. 'I sense little people,' she said.

'Can you see them, Gran?' asked Edie. 'The *koti* . . . *koti* . . . *ton* . . .'

'The *kotitonttu*? No. No!' said Granny Agata. 'Not any more. But I still know if they are there. And that's enough for me.'

'It's time for the Christmas lights,' said Edie, and she nodded at Impy, who let out a piercing whistle.

A small cloud of glowing lights like a flock of luminous starlings made its way over from the Hillside Camp and hovered in front of the four humans on the platform. The flits had created an improvised light show by each carrying a lit birthday cake candle or a twist of reflective silver foil, a miniature torch or a luminous bead that glowed in the dark. Jot and Speckle flew up to join them and the flits started to move, circling, gliding and looping the loop. Their lights flickered and sparkled like a firework display in slow motion. Even Granny Agata, who couldn't see the flits, could see the lights of the flickering cake candles and the luminous beads dancing above her.

'This is amazing,' said Naz. 'Why did you never tell me about them?'

'You wouldn't have believed me.'

'Yeah, you're right. I suppose I wouldn't,' she laughed.

'You won't tell anyone?' asked Edie.

'Never,' said Naz, rubbing her hands to keep warm. 'I promise.'

Edie felt a familiar tickle as Impy lodged herself in her plait.

'Can you hear me?' Impy whispered in Edie's ear.

'Yes. Yes, I can,' Edie whispered back.

'It's your birthday this week, isn't it?' Impy said.

'Yes, I'm twelve on Christmas Eve.'

'So you won't be thirteen for another year?'

'No,' Edie said firmly.

'That's good.'

They lapsed into silence as all four humans and one flit gazed up at the tiny glimmers of light electrifying the night sky.

Thank you for choosing a Piccadilly Press book.

If you would like to know more about our
authors or our books, or if you'd just like to know
what we're up to, you can find us online.

www.piccadillypress.co.uk

And you can also find us on:

We hope to see you soon!